AF405895

PRAISE FOR JUNIPER

'Sun-scorched and bleached, Juniper is a town where the people have turned inwards. What's cooking during the long hot summer of deprivation is particularly unsavoury. Ross Jeffery has birthed the lovechild of Stephen King and Cormac McCarthy.'

-Priya Sharma-

'Juniper is one vivid town on the edge of active desperation; this novella is an intense, effective read.'

-Aliya Whiteley-

'Deliciously dark and delightfully peculiar, this wildly original story of small-town America is both disturbing and beguiling. Jeffery injects a rich stream of humour into the vein of his prose, and doesn't flinch in producing images that stay embedded in the mind's eye. The result is a story that jumps off the page and grabs you by the throat, sometimes veering towards absurdity before swerving back into sheer terror. Richly inventive, compulsive, and with a strong and distinct voice, it is grotesque, often repulsive, and I loved it.'

-Lucie McKnight Hardy-

'Ross Jeffery's *Juniper* is not for the faint of heart. Visceral and raw but always poetic, Jeffery successfully channels Chuck Palahniuk and Stephen King at their shocking best. You'll want to look away at times, but trust me when I say, you won't dare turn your back on Juniper.'

-Daniel James-

'*Juniper* reads like the demented offspring of Burke's *Kin* and Ahlborn's *Brother*. Hypnotic with his writing, Jeffery grabs the reader from page one. The element of the unknown festers throughout this book and makes for a truly unnerving read, one that will make you continue to turn the pages – un-put-downable! One of the best books I've read this year.'

-Steve Stred-

'*Juniper* is an atmospheric portrait of a ravaged town—a town full of grotesque brutality, but also full of character and colour and the energetic struggle for life in the midst of destruction.'

-Naomi Booth-

'The Southern Gothic collides with Grand-Guignol in this timely, highly original, R-rated novella exploring the survival instinct in both humans and animals. Brilliantly atmospheric and undercut with pitch black humour, be warned: JUNIPER is not for the faint of heart - there are scenes in it that will stay with you...'

-Sarah Lotz-

Tome

Scorched

Milk Kisses and Other Stories

Only The Stains Remain

Tethered

Beautiful Atrocities

The Devil's Pocketbook

Cover Art: Daniele Serra

Cover Design: Ross Jeffery (Paperback)

Cover Design: Chad Lutzke (Hardback)

Interior Illustrations: Ryan Mills

Book Layout: Ross Jeffery

JUNIPER

THE JUNIPER SERIES
BOOK ONE

ROSS JEFFERY

CONTENTS

To my darling wife Anna

- My Favourite and My Best -

I REMAINED TOO MUCH INSIDE MY HEAD AND ENDED
UP LOSING MY MIND.

-EDGAR ALLAN POE-

CHAPTER ONE

I t was the summer that everything burned.

The sun scorched the land, the soil cracking like warm brownies out of an oven. Juniper was a small, rural town; a waste product of a town, clinging to life from its bordering sibling states. Juniper struggled with being an underdeveloped place, starved of support from neighbouring states and crippled by its shared status in the cramped womb of Southern America – it was incompatible with life and that was sugar-coating things.

You wouldn't find it on any map, try as you might, because it seemed to evade those looking for it, hidden within a crease; untraceable, like floaters in the eye. Juniper was a forgotten pissant town, a town which none of the bordering states wanted to claim ownership of; its existence was an abhorrent reminder of all that was wrong in the world. They'd rather it suffocate and fall out of existence. But Junipeans were made of sterner stuff, and they always found a way to survive.

It seemed that sickness and trouble always seemed to be brewing within its boundaries, causing those that escaped Juniper's clutches to state it was cursed; a town only fit for the dying or incarcerated, a place where hope went to die. The town boasted its fair share of racists and fascists, and claimed to have the highest rate of suicide in America; add to that a dilapidated and failing prison, where the powers that be sent prisoners that they simply wanted to disappear (because who'd look for them in a shit-hole town that everyone wanted to forget?). That's not to mention the Biblical flooding a few months prior to the scouring heat – which was now boiling the town into a frenzied mess.

Juniper, for all intents and purposes, was circling the drain - there was no doubt about it. But the townsfolk were persistent, clinging onto their existence like ticks on a cow. Parasites, sucking all they could from it, becoming bloated in greed and dishonesty, growing spoiled by the town's malevolent soul, until they detached, swollen and spoiled, either to the grave or by punching their ticket to another state, claiming a better life existed elsewhere, anywhere other than here.

So Juniper, for those that still lived here, just existed; a festering boil, clinging to the butt-cheek of those surrounding southern states; each turning a blind eye, refusing aid, neglecting the townsfolk, waiting for this cyst of a town to be lanced and drained from existence. Juniper wasn't always like this, but sometimes you can't beat the hand you're dealt, or polish a turd. Crops failed, hopes faded, and the prison – the biggest employer in the town – had been investigated for gross negligence a few years back, a fact that threatened to close the whole place down. If things weren't bad enough with that hanging over the town like a hangman's noose, the flooding of a few months back had wiped out the only industry this town had: farming. So, what could generations of Junipeans do? What could the townsfolk who only knew how to farm the land do, when there was no land left to farm?

Juniper just kept on keeping on, blindly following a trajectory that was pointed straight down. The town was crashing and now burning before the residents' very eyes. They were abandoned, and each person in Juniper was quietly awaiting the inevitable cataclysmic event which would raze this sorry place to the ground and end their misery.

The flooding that preceded the heat they were now embroiled in destroyed the infrastructure of the town. They'd tried to survive it, the flood; sandbag barricades hastily built in construction lines by prisoners from the local penitentiary, about the only good they ever offered. The town square became a disaster relief zone, an image like one so often seen on the television screen, hailing from some far-flung country. They'd called for more help, but the calls were never answered, and so they did their best.

The farmers were busy trying to save their livelihoods and livestock. Being an agricultural town, it was how the townsfolk had been able to survive all these years. But by the time they'd finished battening down the hatches, leashing their cattle, it soon dawned on them that all the sandbags would be gone. So, instead of wandering into town with hope, they hunkered down and prepared for the end of days.

The poor and unprepared, who accounted for most of Juniper, would be left outside with no ark to come to their rescue. People clambered over one another for help, drains backed up, a frisson of dread hung in the air like the noisome smell of raw sewage that spilled forth on the land.

There was talk at one point of calling in the National Guard, if things continued to spiral out of control – the destruction and devastation left after Hurricane Katrina in New Orleans still fresh in the memory, and the cost of putting that shit right weighing heavy in the pocket of the government. But calling in the guard would mean someone had to acknowledge their existence and pick up the goddamn phone. The town council knew their calls would go unanswered, much like their prayers. If Juniper did succumb to this new trial, if it was swept away by the flood, destroyed like Sodom and Gomorrah, would anyone really bat an eyelid?

Just when they thought the rain was the worst the gods could do to them, then came the fire; and those on the outskirts were left to fend for themselves.

Betty Davis was one such outlander. She had an old shack out by the 701, the only place around for miles. The young folk of Juniper used to throw stones at her window and call her a witch, in part due to her disheveled appearance, but also because she seemed to be ageless, albeit haggard. Betty just kept on going. The name-calling she actually enjoyed; it meant people saw her, that she was still worthy of conversation. She embraced the persona of a witch, especially during the month of October. But most of the time she was left to get by with what she had, which wasn't much, she was a person of simple needs and even simpler pleasures.

Betty was the sole sentry at the edge of town. She had worked the fields with her husband until his untimely death. Since his passing the farmstead had wasted away, the soil untilled, the crops left to wither and die. She couldn't keep the place afloat - so she sold some of the land to other farmers, made a killing, right before the land was made worthless by the pestilence ravaging it now. As Betty didn't have a farm to run, she had plenty of time on her hands. Wanting to keep busy, she spoke with the town council and they bestowed on her the job of keeping the town's population board current. With so many old and infirm in town and with its high death toll (suicide aside), instead of investing in a sign they simply gave her number cards to change when they sent her their weekly message, cards informing her who had died that week. Sometimes she felt as though she was keeping score at a baseball game, but it at least kept her busy and occupied.

Betty was shuffling her way down the 701. The ground had opened up, as the skin of a burn victim tends to, the spent liquid evaporating in the heat. Deep grooves made her journey even more treacherous, what with her hip not being what it was. The grooves were revealed where the earth had separated: sucked of all its moisture, skin losing its elasticity, pulled apart, singed and curled at the edges by the heat.

The earth was hard where months before it had been a bog.

Scorched.

A wasteland.

As Betty trundled along she sucked on a piece of corn, to keep her saliva running and to stop dehydration setting in; it also prevented her sand dune of a tongue from sticking to the roof of her mouth. She recalled as if from a dream the name Jud Dibbers. He was able to spit corn into a hat from well over twenty feet; he was in the Guinness Book of World Records, until someone from Mantiowoc County beat him by another two feet and then he and Juniper disappeared from memory. For a fleeting moment she'd forgotten what had happened to Jud Dibbers, but then she remembered hearing about him growing depressed, ended up painting his shed brain-grey with a shotgun. It sent a chill down her spine, which was odd, considering the heat that now ravished her body.

Ash swirled up from the ground in the humid summer breeze. It was a breeze that was so hot it felt heavy, a heat that would leave its mark on anyone caught out in it. The ash undulated in the air, falling in a blanket of ripples, as if someone had just disturbed a body of water. The white dust of burnt vegetation swept through the town, along with literal wild fire.

As the weather became more unruly, so did the people. Betty glanced at an abandoned car on the 701, a banged-up Dodge Charger; most of the windows were smashed, but the windscreen was still intact. Someone had scribbled a picture of a hand flipping the bird on it, and just in case you didn't get the message, a *Fuck U* next to it. These etchings in dust were all over Juniper. On cars and windows, any pane of glass became a canvas on which Juniper's illiterate children (or what was left of them) and quite possibly a few adults could scrawl their obscenities; a few dicks, some tits, all manner of monstrosities. It was the talk of the town for a while – not the dicks or the tits, but when it would rain. Something, anything to dampen the dust down, help the farmers stay in business, help the town survive.

As well as being a farming town, Juniper also had a roaring hunting trade, dealing in pelts, meat, even bones – they'd trade anything they could catch. But since the flooding and the heat, the hunters of Juniper were now complaining too, because there was nothing left to hunt. The torrential rain of the previous months had driven most of the wildlife out, the devastating flooding destroying their homes.

Then the unrelenting heat burned up what remained. You'd think that the forests would have had a hard time burning, given the rain, but the trees went up like kindling beneath a match.

People were going hungry, those that hadn't fled; their previously full bellies now pickled by copious amounts of moonshine, and even that was running out. Many a family in Juniper survived on what they could grow, hunt, trap, or catch, but now there were withered fields, and hunting expeditions most often than not ended in empty traps and empty stomachs.

Betty stopped as something rustled nearby in the forest. She turned expectantly, hoping to see something she could eat, maybe a rabbit; she'd have no way of catching it, but it would have been a sign, a totem, something to suggest life was returning to Juniper. As she continued watching, a branch fell from up on high, finally giving in to the unrelenting heat, collapsing and then shattering into pieces as it hit the ground; made brittle by the lack of water, and adding as it landed to the blanket of charred flora that had already succumbed to the devastating heat.

Last summer, Betty recalled, they were shooting buck for fun out by old Brandenburg's estate. Jerry, the head of the town council said it was *'rich pickins'*. Said *'the bucks were just asking for it'* - walking out bold as brass, wanting to be mowed down by a hail of bullets.

Trucks rolled into town that summer laden with bucks. There were carcasses piled high in every wagon, blood sloshing around, dripping out around the tailgates, leaving a bloody trail from the forest to the square. The road into Juniper was stained red that summer.

The council had said that they'd gone too far, that they'd raped the forest, torn its creatures from the womb that nurtured them. That the hunters had desecrated something sacred, mortally wounded it in some way, that they'd reap what they'd sowed...

Maybe they were right.

But now, with the town in the throes of death – first by flood, now by fire – life in Juniper had found a semblance of existence. Or at least surviving. Whatever way you looked at it: the town was fucked.

The first thing to go was the harvest. It had been laid low by flooding and then wildfire, a blight that corrupted the very soil. The lakes and rivers were next, first over fished, then dried up with the subsequent heat. Now all that remained were fetid muddy puddles with the remnants of dead or dying fish.

The townsfolk in these harsh climes had become resourceful, however. Those who were obdurate became sick, or lame, or eventually perished; those that chose to survive, survived.

Whatever it took.

CHAPTER TWO

Betty, always frugal with her dwindling savings from the sale of some of her farmland, now survived on roadkill. It was slim pickings at best, but needs must when the devil's driving. It's what brought Betty to the 701 today: a once blacktopped road which – after years of neglect and the state not wanting to claim responsibility for its upkeep - had now turned into a potholed dust track that cut its way through Juniper like a jagged scar. She'd had some luck of late, partly due to her being the only soul out this far. It seemed that any animal that was mowed down on the outskirts of town or gave up the ghost due to the scorching solar glare belonged to her in some archaic way.

Today was like no other; she hobbled down the edge of the 701 pushing her wheelbarrow, her head shrouded with a shawl to protect her balding scalp from the heat of the sun. The barrow served as her shopping-cum-recycling cart. She'd chuck in the dusty roadkill alongside the discarded paraphernalia of a disposable generation. Now that global warming had turned the world to shit, no one seemed to care about recycling, so people continued to slowly destroy life on this fragile rock she'd called home. But not Betty.

Betty had already collected a few discarded bottles of Coke, warmed in the summer sun, but still tasty and refreshing – like drinking warmed treacle. Betty stooped, picked up a bottle from the barrow and took a swig. It was a taste you had to get used to, and she had; the warm fluid coating her gullet in syrupy delight. She used her other hand to shield her eyes from the intense brightness. Surveying the expanse of road, her land, and the possibilities of food that lay strewn across it.

Bumps in the road signified meals, something to satiate her continual hunger. "*Fast food*", she called it, often laughing to herself. Squashed or desiccated, it didn't matter to Betty because the yearning in her stomach overrode the sight of bluebottles and wriggling maggots. The fire would purify the meat of its ills. She had no choice. If she didn't, she'd die.

A bit further down the road, near the route sign punctured by bullet holes, something lay prostrate on the ground, only slightly visible in the heat wave which duly blurred its edges.

Things still hadn't changed all that much in relation to gun control. If anything, it had gotten worse. People would fire off rounds when speeding through Juniper. There were still shootings in schools and mass murders in the news. They said it wasn't guns that were the problem but people, so Betty thought to herself '*why do they keep giving guns to people so readily, if they're the root of the problem?*'

Betty screwed the lid back on her Coke and threw the bottle into the barrow with the roadkill she'd already collected. She headed towards the bullet-ridden sign. She glanced over her shoulder frequently so as not to be hit by a passing truck and in turn become somebody else's harvest; times were bleak after all.

As Betty approached the mass on the floor, she discovered that it was still breathing. Its body wasn't moving at all, but a strange wheeze emanated from its mangled form. She set the wheelbarrow down, as close as she dared get to this tangle of limbs and bloodied flesh. The sound reminded her of the lambs Hank used to take off to his shed and slaughter... those innocent little beings. The animal-screams of slit throats, all gargled and strained, used to punctuate the air at night during lambing season. The screams were always followed by that same odd, guttural wheezing...

The dust, swept into the air from the forest fires by the odd passing car had blanketed this thing. It'd settled on the blood which had oozed out from beneath it like pus from a festering wound. It had turned the blood into a paste, which had in turn stuck this poor fallen creature where it lay, a fly caught on a strip of sticky tape.

The flies circling the harvest Betty had already amassed in her barrow began to descend, drawn by the smell and the chance of a fresh meal. She had watched their ungodly process many times: first, they spewed over their food, digesting what they could, and then they lay eggs in bored-out holes. The circle of life in all its gory beauty; for these creatures, survival was never in question.

Betty shambled closer to the stricken shape, raspy whimpers seemed to bubble from its mouth. She bent down and reached out an arthritic hand to brush some of the dust off. As she touched it, its damaged head lifted ever so slightly, a sound like Velcro as it peeled itself from the blacktop. She realised in an instant that it was a larger than anything she'd encountered on the road before. A feral-looking ginger tom. Given its size, it must have been doing pretty well up until now; its stomach was large and plump, its limbs, though broken, still visibly muscular.

Betty began to salivate, bringing the back of her hand up to wipe away the spit dripping from the corner of her mouth, imagining how succulent it would taste. *How many meals are lying right there?* she mused to herself, glancing over its rotund body and thick limbs. A catch this size would keep her fed for months.

That was until it looked at her.

Its jaw hung loosely, most likely shattered by whatever had run it down. Betty's eyes met the forlorn creature's. There was some sort of instant connection: she sensed a longing, or pleading, for help. Either it was pleading with her to rescue it, or it was pleading with her to bash its brains in and put it out of its misery... but before Betty could decipher which, she heard the distant rumble of an approaching pickup truck.

Betty shuffled round the stricken tom, cursing her limp all the while. She had her father to thank for that constant reminder. He'd forgotten to cover the well when she was a child. Betty fell nearly twenty foot straight down, landing with a crunch on her left leg. Broke in six places and shattered, like a candy cane dropped on a concrete floor. Dr. Levi said she was lucky to still be alive. He'd do what he could to save the leg, but she'd most probably have a slight discrepancy as she grew. She often thought if she'd known the pain that the discrepancy would cause her back and hip, corrupting her day to day life, she'd have been better off having it amputated in the first place. It would have been better than living her adolescence as a freak, someone all the children feared – being different in a place like Juniper was like a death sentence.

Amputation seemed to be working out alright for the war vets, who sat around smoking and drinking at Sam's Bar. They were regarded as royalty in Juniper, free to do and say whatever they wanted, seeing as they'd left limbs overseas fighting for freedom, losing nonetheless. If Betty had lost a leg, she could have infiltrated their ranks, she could have been their eye candy, and God knew she could have done with the company. She'd missed deep and meaningful conversation since her children had left, and the death of her husband. Betty longed for it, that sense of connection with another, but the absence of it weighed heavy on her like a yoke.

Betty bent down and began scraping the body from the road. It was heavier than she anticipated, and she struggled to separate flesh from the porous blacktop. The pickup loomed ever closer, hurtling down the highway towards them. She needed to get her cargo into the wheelbarrow and stowed before somebody else laid claim to it.

She snaked her arms around the torso and pulled. It made a sound like unwinding duct tape as she yanked the body from its bloody moorings; it let out a strained yelp.

'*I'm trying to save you,*' she offered into the air. '*If they find you...*'

She nodded to the oncoming truck. '...*they'll put you on a spit faster that you could say Shish-Kebab.*'

Betty heaved the limp, broken mass of the tom into her wheelbarrow, her muscles burning as she lifted the dead weight. It fell in with a metallic thud; the barrow almost toppled, upended by the sheer weight of the thing. The pickup was only a few hundred feet away now, plumes of dust and dirt cast into the sky in its wake. Betty began scooping up the legs that dangled over the lip of the barrow. The bones in those legs were like pool balls in a sock. She was struck by the thought of having known that pain herself. She'd see what she could do to salvage the legs; it would be time consuming work to nurse the creature back to life, but time was something she had. She was no medical professional, and this discovery needed to remain a secret; she didn't want anyone sniffing around her prized find, taking away her new found companion before they'd had a time to get acquainted. She'd have to research some medical procedures at the library in town, but that was a worry for another day, and a less pressing time.

Stuffing the mangled limbs and broken body parts on top of the other less fortunate road kill, Betty removed her shawl, feeling the immediate effect of the sun on her skin, evaporating the sweat that had slicked her balding dome. She draped the shawl over the barrow.

'You stay quiet, you hear me? If you know what's good for you,' she whispered.

The truck skidded to a stop, dusting Betty with detritus. She glanced up and saw that it was that fucking reprobate Klein, Janet Lehey's husband. An odd fellow, a man full of childish and ridiculous habits. Some said he was a simpleton, married to an overbearing but popular woman. You see, Janet Lehey had gained some notoriety for keeping the town afloat and stomachs full in this most recent worsening famine – Klein just hung in there, reaping the rewards and filling his fat little rodent-like face.

Klein leant on his door, window down, aviators concealing his weasel-like eyes, his round face showing that food was in great abundance at their table. His lips wrestled with a cigarette as he shuffled it across to the corner of his mouth.

Betty stole a glance at the wheelbarrow, its contents thankfully concealed by her shawl. She hobbled up to the beaten-up Toyota, its paint flecked and peeling, burned off by the heat of the sun and its daily grind.

'What you doin' out here Betty?' Klein took a deep suck on his cigarette.

'I live out here Klein, as well you know. I might be asking you the same question... I'm just getting some takeaway.' A small chuckle made the last few words uttered dance and hang playfully in the air.

'Find anything good?'

'Not much to write home about: couple of tree rats and a pancaked porcupine... you didn't answer my question... why you so far out of town?'

'You know, just checking the lay of the land... Janet lost one of her prized livestock, just seeing if it had wandered out this ways. You ain't seen it, have you? Big fella, could pull down a deer or so I've heard – monstrosity of a cat, looks like he was born in hell! Ring any bells for ya?'

'Nope, not seen nothing... nada.'

Klein finished his cigarette, letting the moment fester between them. Despite his child-like qualities, Klein was a very disbelieving man. Ever since he got out of Juniper Correctional for attempted murder, he'd never been able to trust a soul; seemed like he carried the ghosts of that place with him wherever he roamed, a disquieted unease about him. He never talked about what happened in there and it was probably best those things stayed locked up – Betty imagined that he probably didn't trust his own mind half the time.

Klein flicked the remaining ember of his cigarette to the floor; it landed near the ginger tom's last resting place. He reached up with his stubby nicotine-stained fingers, pulled his aviators down, revealing a weasel brown eye. The other was cloudy, soured milk in colour, from an altercation in the Juniper Correctional with another inmate – over a dispute about a book.

The aviators slid from their perch on a trickle of sweat, over rivers of broken capillaries, all blotchy and swollen. They came to rest at the tip of his bulbous snout. Klein enjoyed a beer more than most, but moonshine was his chosen poison; the amount he drank would be enough to make some go blind, crazy or both. He pointed down to the ground and indicated the congealed bloodstain, heavy with blue-bottles.

'That there... bit more blood than from a squirrel, ain't it...? Or a porcupine for that matter...'

Betty glanced down at the discarded cigarette, hissing within the congealing blood. Her eyes darted to the barrow. She thought she noticed something shift under her shawl. Did Klein see it? Betty's heart was thundering in her chest; at any moment, she thought, Klein would climb out of his cab and take what she'd harvested.

'Half a deer... find of the century wouldn't you say, considering?' Betty waved her had around the apocalyptic wasteland that had become Juniper 'Been fed on though, just got here before it turned bad... anyway, I didn't see nothing down this way, but if I see your livestock, I'll get a message to Janet, you hear?' Betty was trying to hurry the conversation along, the sooner Klein was out of the way, the sooner she'd be alone.

'So why you down here with the 'barra?'

'Like I said, saw some birds down this way so thought I'd check it out, what with this hip...' Betty bashes her hip for emphasis '...need all the help I can get, you know? Well, I best be off, this roadkill ain't gunna skin and cook itself now, is it? You be good now and like I said: you tell Janet that I'll keep my eye out... which one is it this time?'

Klein prodded the glasses back up, concealing his questioning and distrusting eyes. Put the truck in drive and started to move off.

'The big one... Bucky... ginger...you let me know if you see him, ya hear!'

The wheels spun as Klein turned the truck around and headed back into town in a hail of gravel.

Betty waited for the truck's shape to be subsumed by clouds of dust before turning back to the barrow and pulling the shawl away.

'Right, let's get you home and see what we can do! Mamma's going to make you better.'

Betty began the arduous journey back to her shack, fighting the stiffness within her hip, and the sheer weight of the wheelbarrow as it rocked over the gravel and uneven road.

She'd skin the roadkill first and then tend to the ginger tom. Food in this town was so scarce, she needed to eat before someone helped themselves to her harvest.

CHAPTER THREE

Janet tried to keep busy whilst Klein was in Juniper Correctional for beating her to within an inch of her life. She was used to the beatings. Janet had regularly been seen around town sporting black eyes and split lips. After Klein was sent away for the attack that left her near dead, crawling into the town centre with a crimson, broken mess of a face – she looked to put the time she had into other things.

She volunteered and soon started to run Juniper's Baptist Women's Fellowship. It had been well attended, but with the flood and now the drought, numbers had dwindled. In part due to sickness, but mainly in apathy, lethargy at searching, pleading, and imploring God to save them from the plight they now found themselves in.

When this folded, Janet needed something else to put her time into. She soon became resourceful, offering her own form of salvation for those within the borders of Juniper.

The land offered no sustenance: the corn and hops were being ravaged by mice and insects made abundant by the deluge. The other crops had long since perished in the wildfires, and anything that survived those was beaten down until it was withered by the unrelenting sunshine.

So, Janet began breeding cats. Initially, her idea was to keep corn and barley in business: the cats would cull the rodent population. It worked, and the handful of cats that Janet had soon turned into a brood, which grew in turn to a small army of interbred, hulking, furry killing machines. Janet received notoriety and friends, and more importantly: a sense of belonging that had long been withheld from her.

Janet raised cats in the same way she had her children: producing a huge baying mob of a litter, although one point of difference was that the cats stuck around. They cleaved to her, knowing she would care for them, even though her parlour was somewhat frugal.

Janet's children, all seven of them, left town as soon as they could. Some went to university, though heaven knew how they got in. Others just upped sticks and left. Some moved a town or two over, but the others went further afield – fleeing their abusive father's reach and abandoning their mother, the woman who allowed the abuse to happen. They'd called her weak and hated her for her neglect – and so Janet was bereft and alone, all except for her cats.

The children pleaded for Janet to follow them, but she remained by Klein's side, like a loyal beaten mutt. It was the fear of starting over, the fear of being alone that anchored her to him – what could she do, when they'd become entwined over the years? To pull away, like ivy from brickwork, would leave her structurally damaged, so she stayed and let him strangle her bit by bit. Throughout all the beatings, she still loved him. Deep down in her very core there was something that kept her going. Her children called her delusional, but she felt she could change Klein, that she could love the evil out of him. *For better or for worse,* Janet used to say. *In sickness and in health,* was another. *Until death us do part.* Her children wished for that death every day of their lives – but Klein seemed death-proof and clung onto life with an obdurate desire. So, in the end, her children just forgot about her, at least distracted by their own lives. The phone calls pleading for her to come and join them stopped.

Through her breeding program (of the feline variety), Janet created her own form of pest control. But then the cats became their own form of pests to the townsfolk. Her initial small brood of moggies bred, producing even more litters and more mouths to feed. There were so many that the outhouse where she kept them was bursting at its timbers. To the untrained eye, the floor pulsed, as if a large mottled rug was breathing. The cats were penned in and basically savage: feral and hungry. The tiny kittens, at this point born daily, suckled at teats that always left them hungry. The runts of each litter were eaten by their own kind.

Bones and fur littered the floor. The outhouse became both a graveyard and a home. The stronger kittens learned to defend themselves and hunt. They would become the cannibalistic alphas of the brood.

Janet would release the felines at dusk, as the town was shrouded in an autumnal glow. They would run through Juniper hunting in packs like wolves, stalking the mice which were depleting the town of their limited grain stores and what food remained locked behind rickety kitchen cupboards and storehouse doors.

They were in essence doing the town a service, for a time, until the mice began to run out. Then some of the cats turned rabid – foaming at the mouth, bloodlust etched on their retinas, as if seared by a branding iron from hell. There were reports of them creeping into houses, those with newborn children. They were discovered leering at the sleeping babies: tails swinging like metronomes over the sides of cots, mouths open and ready to pounce.

Most would probably let them run free, scatter them to what remained of the fields and forests. Some might consider poisoning the whole rotten lot, to be done with the responsibility. But Janet did neither; for the first time in her life she had a purpose. She was needed, wanted, and adored.

One day, as she'd stood in the sweltering noon sun, the heat slowly cooking her brain, she peered through the cracked glass window of her outhouse building at her brood. Her stomach empty and lips parched, struggling to remember the last time she ate something that gave her sustenance.

Janet swigged from a bottle of moonshine from Klein's now depleted store. Since he had been inside Juniper's Correctional Facility, the manufacturing of their chosen poison had ceased. There was precious little left. Partially blind with the volume of Klein's drink she'd downed, and cooked by the heat, an idea floated into her head of turning the huge baying litter into the new livestock of the town. If the American government wouldn't help them, if Walmart wouldn't support them, if aid wasn't forthcoming – if everyone else had forgotten them – Janet would be the one to make America great again.

She'd feed the town with the new cattle of Juniper.

At first, people were unsure. Although they weren't *their* cats, it still played on their minds – eating what many still thought of as pets. But hunger has a way of turning the most hardened of minds to deplorable acts, and the smell of roasted meat wafting from the Lehey farmstead worked up the townsfolk like sharks caught in a blood-crazed frenzy.

Janet started small, serving her neighbours chunks of delicate meat. The first batch were the medium-sized cats, in-between kitten and hunter. She'd cook them on spits over an old oil drum: coals piled high, hissing with spent fluids and fat as they dribbled onto the inferno beneath.

There wasn't much preparation needed: just a sharp long stick inserted through the body. She'd force the stick through the mouth and push hard until it poked out the other side.

Janet dealt with the brutality of it all by imagining she was darning a garment, perhaps one of Klein's old socks, although sliding the wooden needle through a completely different fabric.

Once the cat was speared, the fire took care of the rest, singeing the hair right off; creating an acrid aroma before it gave way to the usual delicious and intoxicating smell of cooking meat. There was no need for plucking or shaving. Janet span the spit, until the juices had drained and the arms shrivelled in towards the body, becoming hard. The skin shrank and stuck in place as she cooked the cat, rotisserie style, over the drum.

At first, she thought she'd sunk to a new low in her quest to pacify the hunger burning within her, the desire to fill her stomach with more than just moonshine and seeds. Janet thought of herself as an abhorrent monster, partaking in some kind of maternal filicide. But that was crazy: her real children were long gone, the cats just filling a maternal hole and loneliness brought on by Klein's incarceration. He was back now, but Janet knew that a piece of him *didn't* come back. Something else had returned with him in its stead, but she couldn't place her finger on it, and Klein was tight lipped on anything that happened in that god awful place.

The smell and taste of that delicate dark meat became so intoxicating it was irresistible, and the lingering thoughts soon vanished, leaving her numb to the whole grizzly process. At first she hated what she'd become, what she was doing, but after a while, having grown numb to the violence she dished out to these felines, she enjoyed it. She was able to exert her own power over them, much like Klein did to her. She'd get to bash them, break their bones, submerge them thrashing within the waters, hurt them good and proper. It was almost cathartic for Janet, her own private therapy – a way for her to work through her trauma.

Word spread throughout the town, carried on the aroma of cooked flesh. Before long, most of Juniper couldn't get enough of the Lehey delicacy. Those that didn't know about Janet and her cats had their suspicions, but their hunger overrode their search for answers, hunger pulling the words back down before they could be uttered, silencing their inquisitiveness like a knife through a windpipe.

There was one feline that remained strictly off limits. The leader of the pack. Janet's prized stud, as it were: Bucky. The ginger tom. He was a huge muscular beast, the size of a young deer and built like a puma: long powerful legs, lean body, head the size of a spade.

He was the silverback of the group, getting to fuck all the females and slaughter all the would-be suitors. Janet had grown to call her ever increasing litter 'the herd', and Bucky was its ruler. She tried to breed stronger and bigger cats through his seed, so it made sense to keep him off the menu – but this always ended in their slaughter once they came of age, with Bucky ensuring his reign would continue.

One of the reasons he also stayed off the menu was that Janet was scared of him; not that he'd done anything to jeopardise his position in her heart or her enterprise. It was subtler than that: the sly way he sometimes looked at her, sizing her up with that feral rage, plus the stories she'd heard.

Brandenburg told her that he heard a scream one night, loud enough to wake him. Said he almost shit the sheets with fright. He'd jumped out of bed, pulled up his trousers, and slipped his feet into the gaping mouths of his leather boots, grabbing his 12-gauge from the wall.

As well as having a prime hunting spot in Juniper, with his ranch latching onto the green skirt of the forest, Brandenburg kept a small holding of livestock. He'd had more, but hunger and poachers had robbed him of most of it. It was tough work keeping them alive with the famine that was hitting Juniper. Each meal he gave them was food he could be storing, so he'd only kept three goats and a couple of chickens – the goats pretty much tended to themselves and the chickens didn't take too much feeding.

Livestock, actual real-life livestock in Juniper was worth more than money, especially a livestock that produced food. Brandenburg would use the goat's milk to make cheese and butter. His chickens gave him a bounty of eggs, when they felt like laying, which for the last month they hadn't. Those he did find had been hard-boiled. That or he'd find exploded shells and scrambled egg all over the coop.

He'd given much thought to eating them, the chickens, but

decided to give it another month before cutting off the feathered free-loaders' heads.

Brandenburg was more than willing to use deadly force to protect his food supply, which is why he ran out of the house that night with his shotgun in hand. He flicked the porch light on, gun aloft; with no time for pleasantries, no questions to be asked, he began scanning the darkness. If someone was rustling his animals, they would pay with their blood. It was now a matter of life and death. Besides, he used to play ball with the sheriff and had been known to organise hunting parties for the police department on his estate. He was pretty sure that they would turn a blind eye to a self-defence plea.

Brandenburg stood there, clouds of breath pouring from his mouth, surveying his farmstead. There was nothing, only the cold night air scything at his exposed torso. He counted two goats, the chickens were locked up, but where was the last goat?

Brandenburg told folks that, when he was going to turn in for the night – that was when he heard another scream, cutting the air like a sickle. Said he almost discharged the gun. Luckily, he told those listening, it still had the safety on.

After the scream, he'd turned to see something glowing in the tree line: two piercing eyes, glaring back at him. He backed up to his door and reached around for the flashlight near the coat-rack, not for one moment letting his eyes leave the deadlights that stared back at him. Torch in hand, he fumbled with the switch. It burst into light and he said he saw Bucky, staring back at him: face drawn back into a snarl, the skin around its mouth quivering over sharp teeth.

The goat hung from its jowls, neck twisted and contorted.

He fired a shot in the air but Bucky didn't move. The thing just stood there, defiantly judging him. Brandenburg said how his wife and daughters came running down the stairs at the sound of the shot, shock on their faces. He turned to warn them off, and when he looked back Bucky was gone. The goat too.

Janet had always denied it was Bucky. She wasn't about to give up her prized asset, her stud. There was a part of her that recognised she'd been a fool, that she'd reared this beast that was now out of her control. But she buried that secret, told no one about her own fears. She told herself: thousands of Americans kept dangerous animals. Chimpanzees, snakes, spiders. So surely, she could handle a cat?

But with him missing, now, she felt uneasy, afraid. He'd turn up eventually, she had no doubt about that, but with what kind of offering? That was the real question that kept her up at night.

CHAPTER FOUR

As flesh and bone were separated, white and bright, Betty tossed arms and legs into the black pot that her mother had given to her: a relic passed down from woman to woman, all the way back to her great-grandmother, who'd stolen it from a family off fighting in the Civil War.

Betty went about the work like a qualified butcher: twisting limbs from joints with a *pop*, pulling musculature from the skeleton, sorting the tendons and veins. There was skin and pelt splayed over her table, beginning to curl at the edges. There was a roaring fire on, which crackled and popped as the corpses she worked on did likewise.

Betty pulled the meat cleaver from its resting place atop the wooden bench, and with one arcing slash the head was loosed from the body, producing a sickening crunch.

Betty brushed the head aside with the flat edge of the cleaver, sweeping it off the table and into the slops bucket, where it landed with a squelch. It wasn't rocket science, but skinning and preparing animals had a dance to it, a methodical sway, and rules that needed to be observed and followed. Betty, in her hunger, had given up on such things. She needed food, and needed it now.

She slit the limbless and headless torso from throat to anus. Placing her hands, mottled in fur and blood, into the incision, she inverted the corpse over the slops bin. Organs and liquid escaped and dropped with a wet slap into the bucket. The smell there seemed to permeate, no cleaning product on Earth able to remove it. As it wandered up into her nostrils, she rubbed her nose against her shoulder and stifled a gag.

Betty wondered what in high hell these things had been eating, as the remnants of its stomach came falling into the bucket. It was enough to make her contemplate whether she should eat it at all, but her stomach grumbled its desire. She put the thought aside, and prepared herself.

Betty continued chopping the eviscerated torso on the table with scything strikes from the cleaver, dicing the body into small chunks. She stood, then wandered over to the larder, poking her head within. She realised what she had already known. There was nothing to add to the pot; she was living literally hand-to-mouth. She returned to the kitchen, grabbed some herbs from the sideboard: rosemary and thyme. Nearly dead, they crumbled in her fingers, but would add some flavour at least.

Betty dropped the diced meat into her ancient black pot, along with the severed limbs and bones. She rubbed the herbs together in her hands, blowing it over the pink flesh. Her mouth was full of wetness. She moved to the sink and poured in water, pinched some salt and pepper and sprinkled it into the watery mix. She hobbled over to the fire, placing the pot on the hook, swinging it over the blazing coals.

With dinner bubbling away, Betty shambled back into the living room: a dusty crammed place. It was full of rugs, animal skins, and hunting trophies; bright white, near-bleached skulls adorned three of the four walls. The fourth partition was somewhat a rogue's gallery. Pictures adorned every available space: sepia, black and white and coloured photographs showing how time was shifting, dead family staring out at her from every frame.

Betty would sit for hours, staring at the photos of a time gone bye. Since her husband had died she'd been alone, bereft of friends and loved ones, so she'd stare at the wall for so long she'd grown to know it intimately: every indentation, every drip of dried paint, every insect she'd hit with a slipper.

Reminiscing and cursing, remembering and crying.

Betty often thought to herself that it wasn't the dead that suffered loss but those who were left behind to carry on, those that were left to finish the race. She shuffled into the room, removing a small box from her apron. She struck a match, and then set about lighting the many candles that were placed around the room. She shuffled around, carrying the flame between each candle, the room blossoming into a warm orange glow. Now that the sun was gone, descended behind the mountains, the air outside had turned cold as the Juniper River in winter, enough to take the breath away.

The room came alive with the flickering carrot-coloured light. Betty blew out the match and placed it on the mantelpiece next to a plethora of other blackened matches. A photo of her husband stood next to this odd collection. She reached out and pulled it toward her, brushed the dust from it and kissed it.

'You daft old man, why did you have to leave me? Why didn't you ask for help? I told you that doing everything yourself was gunna get you killed. You had to prove me right, didn't you, you silly old fool.'

Betty placed the picture back on the mantelpiece and walked around the couch sitting in the middle of the room. It was lumpy as an acne-ridden face, but damn was it comfortable. Betty slept on it more nights than she cared to remember, drinking moonshine until the early hours, talking to ghosts in frames, and the ghosts who appeared at her door.

She waddled around the arm of the sofa and dropped into the seat, dust billowing into the air. She'd given up on appearances a long time ago. Plus, no one ever came out to see Betty, unless they were coming to hurl stones or insults. Even then, she didn't get to see them.

They hid in the shadows of the night, always at the edge of her failing eyesight.

As she relaxed back on the sofa, her body sinking into the plump cushions, her eyes fell on what was laying before her.

'So, my little dar'lin, what's momma going to do with you?'

The ginger tom was crumpled in a heap where she'd left it, a huge, sprawling and bloodied mess on the rug, mangled, yet clinging to life; despite everything, it kept breathing.

'Let's clean you up a bit, shall we? Momma's gunna make you all better, don't you worry your little fuzzy head about it...' She lent forwards and ruffled the matted, bloodied hair on its head.

CHAPTER FIVE

Klein had arrived home hot and bothered after searching for Bucky. His shirt was sodden and stuck to his back like a new skin. The leather seats of his car and the lack of air conditioning made sure he was one hell of a slippery mess when he clambered out of the pickup and walked towards his house.

Klein lived like he always had to make up for what he lacked in height; always with a cock-sure attitude. But he was the kind of guy that, if he'd been tall and strapping, would probably be angry with everyone that was shorter than him. The rage which burned within him was unquenchable and unyielding; it got him in trouble from time to time and resulted in him being locked up in Juniper Correctional.

The screen door was closed but the front door wide open. When Klein stepped inside it was like an oven, the corrugated steel roof drawing down and holding the heat in long after the sun slipped behind the mountains.

It was at times as if he were living inside a slow cooker. Klein even thought that when he woke up in the mornings he'd tanned overnight. He threw his keys into the bowl by the front door and strutted from room to room, trying to locate his wife.

'Janet!' The lounge was a mess: newspapers and fans working overtime, cables strung across the floor and over chairs like tree roots trying to find water; anything to abate the unrelenting heat. More often than not these attempts at cooling the house were reminiscent of opening an oven door, the fans blowing scalding heat into the opener's face.

'Janet... where the hell are you?'

He moved into the office, a place that when he was incarcerated had become a room of comfort for Janet, where she would like to waste her time, reading books and doing paperwork, sorting out the bills and monies owed to keep the "farm" going. In the corner were boxes of Klein's junk piled high in unsteady stacks, waiting for a strong breeze to knock them down like a child's building blocks. They'd been packed up when he was serving time and since being out he'd not bothered to unpack them.

Klein moved into the study and then through the other door into the kitchen. He stomped over to the fridge, lifting the handle up with a click. The cool air was a slap to his hot face. He extracted a can of beer and rubbed it across his brow. He slowly turned, backing his body up to the cool air tumbling from the fridge, his backside almost resting on a plate of cold feline meat. He held the door open with one arm, and wedged himself in the fridge.

Finally cool enough to think, Klein lifted the can to his mouth, searching out the ring-pull with his buck teeth. He pulled open the can, and it sprayed his face with foam. Klein didn't give a shit. He slurped up the foam and necked half of the underlying beer.

Pulling himself out of the fridge, he slammed the door closed behind him, bottles clinking inside with the force. He strode over to the kitchen window, overlooking the outhouse. Klein knew that if Janet wasn't in the house, she'd be out there, tending to her livestock.

There she was, a bucket of cooked cat in one hand and a leg in the other; chow time. He rapped his knuckles on the window pane so hard the glass shook and creaked in its frame, threatening to break. Janet turned to see Klein staring back at her with rage in his eyes. She held up one hand, the one with the leg in it, mouthing *one minute.*

Janet went over to her cattery and flung a few pieces of meat from the bucket in through the window. Klein could hear her baying brood mewling and meowing as they devoured their own brother, sister, mother, cousin – who knew?

The cats still needed feeding, especially now the rodent population was in decline, and as Janet had discovered, they were more than happy eating their own. Why waste their other meagre supplies on fattening them up only to slaughter them later to feed her growing demand of clients?

Klein heard Janet walk in through the back door, the screen door banging closed. He hid. Caught the sound of the bucket as it landed on the floor with an empty clang. He could sense her movements as she wandered gingerly into the house, wary of him. Her breathing short and shallow. Fear pulling at her outward composure, like a strand of thread from a jumper.

'Klein... Klein where are you?' She spoke with a fractured voice, each word sounding as though it was going to crumble away into dust. Janet noticed his beer can on the table. She moved towards the sink to wash her bloodstained hands. She could sense something was going to happen, noticed a darkening shadow and a looming presence behind her. She turned to discovered Klein bearing down on her, his milky eye weeping slightly as he gripped her by the throat with one chubby paw. Janet's hands shot up to wrestle with the arm choking her. But though he was short, he was still immeasurably stronger than her when he was in a rage. A cigarette nestled in the corner of his mouth, smoke billowing from his lips and dancing over his eye like a grey tongue, like a salamander licking at his eyes.

'Where the fuck have you been?' he spat, pushing her head back against the kitchen cupboard, hand vice-like around her throat. Even if she'd wanted to answer, she couldn't: he was crushing her vocal cords.

'Answer me, you whore, I asked you a goddamn question! Where. The. Fuck. Have. You. Been? You send me out looking for Bucky, in the heat, driving all over Juniper, and you're swanning around here without a care in the world... who you been talking to? Who you been seeing.... hey? Answer me? Or, I swear to God you gunna get another ass whooping. I'll make sure that you won't walk straight for a week.' Klein let go of her throat. Janet crumpled to the floor, heaving and gasping, dizzy from the sudden influx of oxygen. She pulled her legs to her chest, foetal.

'I... I... I was... just...'

'I know you been lying to me...' his mouth foaming, angry and crazed like a rabid dog. 'You just wait until I find that guy you been fucking out there in that barn!' He crouched, his shadow falling over her like a veil.

'You need to be taught a lesson, Janet, you need to be brought back in line again....'

'No, no, I didn't...'

'You think I want to do this? You think I like it?' He was hysterical now. 'Tell me who you been seeing and I won't lay a finger on ya.' It sounded, for all the world, like he was begging her.

'I'm not seeing anyone!'

'I don't want to hear it you filthy slut, now give it to me!'

Klein reached forward and Janet flinched, recoiling from his chubby nicotine-stained fingers. She tried to wriggle away. Klein struck her hard across the face with the back of his left hand, a loud crack ringing out. Her head bounced off the cupboard below the sink. Klein brushed aside her flailing arms, latching onto one. He pulled it taut, and with the other hand he pushed up the sleeve of her shirt, baring her forearm: pockmarked, blistered, scarred.

'No please Klein... I didn't do anything...'

'Listen here, you little bitch, you got ideas above your station. You need to remember who's in charge... I got out of jail and now you think you're some kind of saviour? Some kind of local celebrity? You ain't. You just some filthy whore I keep around the place out the goodness of my heart! Now stop wriggling, you're only going to make it hurt more!'

Janet sobbed.

Klein took a deep drag on his cigarette, the tip a bright burning ember. He let the smoke plume from his nose, a demon with fury stoked in its heart. He took the cigarette from his mouth and pressed the ember-like tip into her flesh. It hissed. Janet stifled a scream – concealing as best she could her hurt. She didn't want to give Klein the satisfaction. The skin blistered and burst, as Klein extinguished the cigarette on the wound. He stood, flicked the cigarette butt at her; it bounced off her face and landed on the floor.

'Now, clean this shit up and get dinner on the table. I need a fucking bath.'

Klein turned and swaggered out of the kitchen, leaving Janet on the floor, collapsed in on herself, like a house that'd just withstood a hurricane.

After his bath, Klein sat at the table; Janet opposite him. She'd prepared feline steak and creamed potatoes with freshly baked rolls. An exorbitant feast by Juniper's standards. More than most households would see in a month. The potatoes sat in a bowl, steam rising from the buttery sauce. An uneasy silence added pressure and weight to a room that already felt suffocating, like the heavy air that rolled in before a thunder storm.

Klein reached over to grab the moonshine from the jug near Janet. She startled at the movement. Klein noticed, sniggered to himself. Janet flushed red.

She'd often thought of poisoning his food, but if he found out, if he caught wind of her devious plan, he'd kill her. She knew he wouldn't even miss a beat.

He'd tried to kill her before, beating her head with an iron poker. That's what had earned him his time, not the countless other beatings. When he got out early, they called it *good behaviour*.

Janet had been told he was a changed man. She mused to herself that he was. He'd returned even more cunning, vindictive, and unstable. She'd never utter these thoughts out loud however; that would be a death sentence. She took the beatings and prayed for God to smite him, strike him down with cancer or a heart attack. She was still waiting.

'Took a drive out to Betty's today. That daft old cow's still collecting roadkill, can you believe that? Surviving on squirrel and porcupine.'

Janet let the sentence drift into the room, amidst her own suspended death sentence. She reached out for the bowl of greens sitting next to Klein on the table. He grabbed her outstretched wrist.

'You hear me woman?'

'Yes... I just thought it was a statement, I...'

'Don't you get smart with me, talking all fancy like. Next time, it'll be your face... do you understand?'

'Yes, Klein, I understand.'

Klein released his grip, throwing her arm back as though he were disgusted by touching it.

He seemed satisfied, returning to shovelling his mouth with cat and potatoes, like an engine hungry for coal; he washed it all down with deep gulps of moonshine. Janet hated the way he ate. It reminded her of a pig. She poured some greens onto her plate.

'How was Betty? Not seen her for a while.'

'She's okay. Seemed quite taken aback about seeing me out there, like she was hiding something. Told her about Bucky being missing, so hopefully she will keep her eye out if he shows up out there. I guess he must have been going further afield to hunt.'

'I guess she doesn't get many visitors living so far out of the town, must get quite lonely?'

'No, I guess not... daft bat don't got no electricity either! Must be going stir crazy out there: no TV, no internet, no fucking fridge or lights.'

'Do you think... would you mind if I went out there to see her?'

Klein dropped his knife and fork onto his plate with a clatter, eyeballing Janet, and took another swig of the moonshine. His milky eye started to weep like a wound might exude pus. He lifted a thumb, caressing the milky substance away. He examined the white pearl on the end of his digit, then wiped it on breast of his shirt.

'Don't see why not? It's a long walk though.'

'Well I thought I could use the...'

'Don't be fucking stupid! You ain't wasting gas driving all the way out there...'

'But you...'

Klein smashed his fist onto the table. The crockery and cutlery rattling with his defiant gesture.

'You questioning me woman? What have I told you about questioning me?'

'No... no... you're right. I can walk. It'll do me good.'

'Too right it will do you good. You starting to look like you need some exercise, all this rich living taking its toll on you!'

'Okay... can we spare a cat? I just can't bear the thought of her eating road kill when we have so much to spare.'

'This ain't a fucking charity Janet. You don't see anyone else giving out handouts... do you?'

'What if I gave her one of the runts, they only get eaten by the larger cats, we wouldn't miss one?'

'OK. Give her a runt. A scrawny one though, all fur and bones... She can make a fucking stew or something. I find out you gave her anything else it will be the belt again, you hear me?'

'Yes Klein, thank you. I'll head over that way tomorrow.'

'I'll find out, you hear me? I always find out. Just you make sure you don't go giving her anything I ain't approved. Now, let me eat my fucking dinner, Florence Nightingale.'

CHAPTER SIX

The mornings in Juniper were when people got shit done. The scorched land was temporarily relieved from the heat, covered with sprinklings of light dew, which would soon be evaporated into an early morning mist. The sweet spot was between 5am and 9am when the sun had yet to rise above the hills and mountains that shielded the town from the harshness of the coming day.

The mountains stood guard, protecting the town with their unwavering shadows. Yet, now they seemed powerless. Had Juniper offended the gods of this world? Had it taken too much from nature, and was nature now taking back what it was owed? Had the mountains turned their giant backs on the quaint town, committing its folk to endure unbearable heat, wild fires, the death of all their agriculture? Were the mountains in fact besiegers, starving them out? Had some offering failed? All people really knew was that the town would die long before these colossuses of ore and granite tumbled from their thrones.

The 701 was clear, the road empty of travellers. Except one.

Betty was on her way into town, dressed for all weathers like the crazy eccentric woman the town had grown to love but avoid where possible. Her shawl wrapped around her shoulders and creeping up at the back, shrouding her head. A cardigan hugged her body, concealed under a wax jacket. She also wore a pair of threadbare trousers dotted with mismatched patches, which were tucked into the top of her hiking boots. She was prepared for whatever should arise. Whether that be hurricanes, scorching heat, or what many thought was the oncoming apocalypse – what with all the natural disasters that the Earth seemed to be birthing with greater and greater frequency.

She had one purpose this morning: getting to the library on Fleet Street. It was one of the oldest buildings in town, a domineering grey structure with huge windows that allowed light to pour in. It was a rather grand building for such a small town, but it gave credence to the value of knowledge, or rather, the value that'd once been placed on it. Grey statues of the town's founders stood outside the library with arms outstretched, welcoming people in. Beneath these statues were plaques dedicated to those townsfolk who went off to fight wars in foreign lands and never came back, or returned but were still waging unseen wars in what remained of their bodies and minds.

It had become a landmark where Juniper's veterans would sit, drink, and slowly cook in the sun, until the sheriff or someone else moved them on. They'd hobble away on crutches, and legs made of wood or plastic. Some would slip away in wheelchairs, only to resurface later and start drinking and reminiscing again. Betty was always kind to these folks. Her father once told her: *'You've got to be kind to everyone you meet Betty, because everyone is fighting a battle you can't see.'*

The town appeared to grow outwards from this building. For many, the library was the heart and soul of the town – it had been there since the beginning, and it seemed would be there until the very end.

Betty's head felt as though it were fighting phantoms this morning. She'd spent the evening tending to the tom. Washing his wounds, Betty had observed his hind quarters as she dabbed him with warm cotton wool, noticing the rather large testes resting on his legs. Definitely a boy, no question about it!

He must be a prime specimen, she'd thought to herself, tending as best as she could to its face; the jaw smashed and split in two. It tried to talk to her in the night, but only stifled yapping sounds emerged from his throat. Two of his limbs were shattered and hung loosely in front of him. She had manipulated his skin, checking for compound fractures hidden within the slew of blood covering his body. She knew about these all too well from when she had her own accident with the well. There had been no puncture wounds on his legs. The bones remained shattered but within their housing of skin.

She'd prodded at its muscular stomach, spending a great deal of time examining the hips. Her hands danced over his prostrate body, caressing it and soothing it with her voice: an old country and western song her mother used to sing to her. Betty's roving hands and soft touch seemed to arouse the tom.

'Who's a big boy then?'

She'd been taken aback, struck by the carnal nature of this animal, how it could be in so much pain but still ready to procreate. Maybe it was one of those strange reactions? She'd heard stories from parents of boys who got erections when they were scared – maybe it was the same here? She personally couldn't relate to the odd phenomenon. Being scared was a sure way to put her *out* of the mood.

Betty had stopped her nursing and soon after fetched a dish. She'd filled it with the meagre nutritional supplies she had: a small amount of milk from the glass jar she kept in the cellar. It was the only place in the house cold enough to store milk and even then, the milk was still mostly room temperature. It was a little lumpy, but *'beggars can't be choosers'*, as she often muttered to herself. She tore some bread from a stale loaf and dropped these pieces into the milk, placing the saucer next to the tom's forlorn and mangled face, noticing as she did, that he had ejaculated over the floor.

'My goodness, we're going to have to get you housetrained, you can't be sloshing your baby gravy all over momma's fine rugs now...'.

He raised his lolling head and inched closer to the dish, hoping to be able to lap at the offering.

'It's OK. Momma's not mad. We're going to get you all mended and put back together, like humpty dumpty, but you are in luck: I don't have hooves for hands.' Chuckling to herself, she stood, extinguishing the candles and then set to reclining on the sofa. There hadn't been much point heading to her bed, so she'd placed her hand down near the tom's face, feeling his panting breaths on her palm.

'Good night, my special little guy. I think I'll call you Tom.'

What should have felt alien felt natural: caring for someone was her purpose in life. Her instincts had surfaced through the clouded and heavy memories of loss and abandonment, rising to the challenge like soldiers that never really lost the ability to fight.

Betty's thoughts before she slept were ravaged intermittently by those of her family, the ones she'd lost and the ones that had fled. She was the sole survivor of a large and ever-present dynasty in Juniper. A whole line of family just erased from the town that gave them birth. She was alone, plagued by her thoughts, which wore her down daily.

She felt Tom lick her hand. It pained him to do so, but through his broken jaw his tongue continued to lap at her hand. Maybe in some strange way he was trying to thank her. It comforted her knowing that she at least had someone that needed her. His licking seemed to erase all the bad thoughts, all the memories, all the years of loneliness, until she fell asleep.

BETTY CONTINUED SHAMBLING along the 701. She'd brought her walking stick with her this time. She didn't like to use it, it made her feel weak and old, but the distance was just too far for her today. She'd almost certainly need to rest up in town before making the journey back. Betty had hoped for a lift, but no one would ever be going out this way, so she quietly resigned herself to a round trip on foot.

Betty neared the outskirts of the town, the sun threatening to break clear of the mountains.

Ahead, Betty could see the Juniper Correctional bus. It was a yellow tube of dented metal on wheels, paint worn and windows barred. Sitting on top, smoking, was the Sheriff's deputy, Barnes.

Barnes was about thirty-two, lived by himself, was born and raised in Juniper, never had an inkling to leave. He wanted to serve the county he was raised in, saw it as his civic duty, having come from a long line of law enforcement officers. He was already the most highly decorated law enforcement worker the Barnes line had ever produced. Although, that wasn't too hard: his other family members were numbskulls. Betty had seen them grow up in town, get the badge and the gun. Instead of doing police business, they would often be off shooting gophers or tin cans in the woods. It still surprised her that a family of incompetent souls could have produced such a fine law enforcement office as the man that now sat before her on the roof of the bus smoking. If he were her son, she'd be proud of his achievements.

As Betty approached, she noticed a rifle nestled in his lap. His hat was pulled low as his eyes scoured the tree line, ready for *something*, but what, she had no idea. Off in the middle-distance, Betty could see two other officers, chewing the fat. She was too far away to hear what they were saying, but they were gesticulating to something in the tree line. That's when five men stumbled out of the small coppice, all clad in Juniper Correctional jumpsuits, carrying bags and long metal sticks with spikes on the end. She was about thirty yards away when she heard Barnes.

'Good morning Betty.' He tugged the front of his hat – Betty thought he was such a gentleman, nothing like his reprobate racist of a father. 'What brings you down this far into town?'

'Need to check some things at the library,' she hollered back, closing the distance as she staggered along the road.

'It's going to be another scorcher today. You better get a shuffle on, don't want you passing out in the heat...shade scuttling away quicker than a bullfrog in summer!'

'I'll be fine, got old trusty here to help.' Betty tapped her stick on the road 'Thank you Deputy Barnes.' She knew his name was Teddy, but she liked to call him by his rank. He deserved it for all that hard work and dedication, after all. 'What are y'all doing out here anyways?'

'We be litter-picking mam. Gotta get these boys some exercise once in a while and the 701 was the best place to start, seeing all the litter out here. It's part of their rehabilitation. Well, that's what the doctors say. Helps them have a focus, giving back to society and all that. If I'm honest, I think it's all psychobabble mumbo jumbo...they should be serving time not making a dime!'

'Oh, they get paid for doing this do they?'

'Yeah, something about their human rights or something.' Teddy jostled his rifle 'Since the coons kicked up such a fuss about slavery way back when, we gotta keep on the right side of the law nowadays... just hold up a sec, mam.' Betty felt disheartened in an instant at his comments; it would seem that Teddy's father's racism had tainted him so, spoiled the good that was in him, that a gibe like this could fall so freely from the young man's mouth.

The shot cracked into the sky; the mountains reflecting the sound back, an echo rippling through the air. The men in jumpsuits stopped moving instinctively, turned slowly on the spot so that they had their backs to the road, and fell onto their knees. They spread their arms wide, as if preparing for crucifixion, holding a trash bag in one and poker stick in the other. The other two officers, awoken from their neglectful chit chat, drew their side arms and pointed them at the inmates on the ground.

'You know the routine guys. You stay down, don't move and let this lady pass, you hear? Don't you even twitch! Eyes down!' Barnes shouted, drowning out the echo of his gunshot. 'Mam, it's all clear for you to pass through: you have a good day now!' Barnes tipped his hat again, his duty fulfilled.

'Thank you, Deputy Barnes. I'll remember you to the sheriff next time I see him. You keep up the good work!'

Betty hobbled onwards, past the bus and the inmates to her left, huge hulking beasts of men. She recognised one, Obadiah Garside - town lowlife, arrested for arson. He burnt down the old town hall. It had been thought derelict, but once the smoke cleared there were three bodies found twisted and grilled in the remains; vagrants most likely, but still, murder was murder any way you sliced it. The others, Betty didn't recognise: some were heavily tattooed, scarred and muscular. They could have been Junipeans, or they could have been out of state convicts; either way, she was glad they were behind her now and under the watchful and dutiful eye of Deputy Barnes.

Betty continued into town, every metre she covered racing with the retreating shadows and the scorching heat that would soon follow.

CHAPTER SEVEN

Janet stood at the kitchen sink, the morning light surging through the window, bathing her in a warm glow. It wasn't the sticky heat of the noon-day sun, but a quite pleasant spring heat. She tried to enjoy it, as it would soon vanish, replaced by a muggy oppressive heat that would boil Juniper in its own filth.

As she scraped and washed what was in the murky water, the sun glinted off something metallic. The flash was so bright it left its imprint on Janet's eyes, even after she tried to blink it away. It remained, persistent and mischievous, like a wasp after jam. She reached a wet hand out of the sink and felt at her neck. There, she found the source of the flash: her crucifix. It had fallen from inside her sweater and was now dangling quite literally by a thread. She quickly pulled it free and sneaked it back inside.

Janet had always struggled with her faith, though she'd been a stalwart of the Baptist church for years. She even got baptised in Juniper as a high schooler, joining the youth set-up and staying in the congregation for a great many years. That was, until she met Klein.

As she stood at the sink scrubbing, her thoughts went to that day, seeing Klein stride across the town square. They were both born in

Juniper and she didn't realise how she could have missed him what with the town being so small, or as the youth called it 'inbred'; but she guessed whilst she was busying herself with church and choir and cross-stitch groups, she'd just been too busy to notice. Klein, in his youth, had been a catch: a little rough around the edges but exotic by Juniper standards. He was to Janet as the apple was to Eve: forbidden fruit. Little did she know then what this slender, attractive and muscular boy would become.

At first, they had been deeply in love, and everybody knew it. They were the golden couple of the town, the talk on everyone's lips. They never spent a moment apart, in the way of all youthful romances. The first time she'd seen his temper flare it was when Jake Kendall was flirting with her. She'd not wanted any part of it, but when Klein turned up and caught Jake trying his luck, he went ballistic, fists were flying – it earned Klein a telling off from the police and Jake a trip to the hospital and a scar that would always remind him of that day. Janet had discovered something else, someone that would fight for her, that would protect her, that would quite possibly die for her. She was smitten; she never knew someone would ever care for her so much. Her love for Klein overflowed – but she was also blinded by her love of him, never seeing the rage he had living inside him as something to fear. How wrong she was. They got married six years later and a child soon blessed their marriage. With the additional pressures of married life, raising a child and tending to the needs of her new husband, God became something she used to know.

Five more children in four years, as if life wasn't busy enough. The God she had abandoned decided to bless them with twins: Maggie and Margo. By this point, Janet already felt like a shell of herself. A wreck. She and Klein were no longer the golden couple, though they were still spoken about.

After the first three children, Klein began to hit the bottle. He was a regular frequenter of the various watering holes in town. He spent the majority of his waking time there, often being thrown out at last orders or getting into scuffles with the other regulars. He'd become well acquainted with the local law enforcement, and in particular Officer Barnes Senior, who would more often than not find him meandering through town, stumbling across roads, bloodied and covered in his own vomit. Barnes Senior would stuff him in the drunk tank to sober up before bringing him home, where Klein would start up the whole sorry affair again, this time on his moonshine. At this stage, his fists would often find his wife.

A song broke through Janet's reverie: John Denver's "Annie's Song". She recalled listening to it when her daughter was born, the first of her six children – when time was a little bit more manageable and peaceful, when she was a newlywed and she could faintly remember what bliss felt like.

Janet began to sing.

As the song broke off into the musical interlude, she saw something moving near the outhouse. It was big, fast, and escaped her roving eyes. Was it Bucky? Had he returned? She was about to head out the door when a crow flew straight into the window. It hit the glass with such force it cracked the pane. She stood on tip toes and watched the crow flounder on the ground before righting itself. It limped around and puffed out its feathers, shook its head disapprovingly at the window, and then took flight again.

She lowered back down from tip-toes, turning her attention to the scar across the glass. She could quite clearly see an imprint of a bird, its oily and dusty feathers splayed out. Janet remembered someone telling her that when a bird hit a window and left its aura behind, it meant that somebody was going to die in that house. She reached a sodden hand up to her neck and fished for her crucifix, offering a silent prayer; for comfort, mainly. She was no longer sure if anyone was listening, it was just instinctive. She laid hold of the cross and played with it between her finger and thumb. Her eyes traced the pattern of the ghost bird on the window, the long wingspan, each feather etched in immaculate detail, imprisoned forever. She followed the wings in to the centre, where the head and beak had perforated the glass. Right in the middle a crack. It had splintered out from the centre in many directions. She glimpsed something then, something that she couldn't look away from; she was rooted to the spot, by fear, and a little by recognition. She could see herself, fractured and distorted in the window, the fractures twisting her appearance. It was still her, but broken and splintered, split what seemed like a thousand times. A thousand versions of herself told her how fragile and pathetic she had become. Each one showed the previous day's wear: a black eye, split lip, and vacant, haunted eyes. Janet moved closer to the glass, her reflection even more grotesque as it magnified with her advance. She could see her reflection's mouth moving, but she was sure hers was not.

Suddenly from within the sink, something shifted and caught her eye, drawing her attention away from her reflection. A bald head, ears flattened, feline in shape, had surfaced in the murky water.

When she glanced back at the reflection, the figure resembled her own sad self, spiralling outward into infinity. She flung water from her hands at the reflection and watched as it rivuleted down, inching its way across the cracks, streaking the window. She placed both hands in the water and withdrew the bald cat.

It was warm but lifeless. Its head lolled to and fro as she shook it dry. For a fleeting moment, it reminded her of Alex. He would have been her sixth child – their only boy and heir to the Lehey farmstead. Only, he'd been stillborn. Janet had held him only for a moment before the midwife took him away. Warm but extinguished of life, as a coal taken from a fire and left to go out. Much like the cat she now held.

In a fit of rage, she slammed the cat down on its back, its lank head clanging off the casserole dish. Taking some string, she bound its feet tightly, as you would do with a chicken, but she used all the strength and aggression one would demonstrate when tying up a hostage. Sprinkled it with salt and drizzled butter across its puckered skin, before placing it in the oven and slamming the door closed.

Janet sat at the kitchen table, the dull ghosts of her past now in bright technicolour. She hadn't realised, but she was fingering the crucifix again. She dug an edge of the cross under her thumb nail, until pain made her relinquish the effort.

It had been a good many years since she'd thought of Alex, and she berated herself for not keeping him fresh in her mind. What kind of a mother could have forgotten their child so easily? But then, perhaps she'd wanted to let it go: place it in a box and leave it on the top shelf.

She reached for her coffee. Noticing her scarred forearm, she recoiled briefly. It was disgusting: ragged and burned, cuts and pock-marks dotting the skin where Klein had sealed the wounds with cigarettes.

The one from yesterday was now a bloody red blister, like mayonnaise mixed with ketchup. The thought made her laugh. What the town wouldn't give for mayo and ketchup. Maybe she could supply them by popping the burn marks on her arms? Her own little vengeful 'secret sauce'.

The laughter subsided. She placed the crucifix back inside her top, sipped her coffee.

'I'm so sorry, Alex. I couldn't help you. The doctors said you were... were... what was it now...' She slammed a hand in frustration on the table; when had things become so foggy? '...incompatible with life. That's it, I couldn't do anything. Please forgive me.' She began to sob, laying her head on her crossed arms at the table, the tears wetting her sleeve.

It was around the time of Alex's birth and subsequent death that Klein was incarcerated at Juniper Correctional. After seeing his only heir vanquished as soon as he'd taken his first breath, Klein blamed Janet for their loss. He blamed her God for not looking after them, for being absent and aloof. He'd beaten her before: for getting home and finding no dinner on the table, for finding holes in his socks that remained un-darned, for not pleasing him with her mouth when instructed to. But the beating he dished out to her three days after Alex's tragic passing was to make all the previous beatings remembered as love taps.

He'd been sitting in his chair by the fire, a bottle of moonshine cradled in his lap, cigarette hanging from his mouth, a vacant expression on his face. Janet had been sobbing since Alex was taken from them. She skulked past the doorway to the lounge, a ghost in her own life, sniffing and holding her hollowed out stomach, Alex's home and eventual grave.

'What are we going to do for the funeral Klein? We ain't got anything to spare.'

'What you talking about, woman?' Klein spat, his cigarette dancing between his thin lips, a snarl etching across his face.

'We need to bury him. We need to pay for the funeral, for the casket.'

'And who's going to have to pay for that, cause you sure ain't got a pot to piss in, have you? You're bleeding me dry, you pathetic excuse for a woman. You can't even do your main function in life. And where the fuck is your God, hey? Where is He, Janet? This God you so adore, more than your own husband, your own children and your dead son! I hear you talking to him. I hear you pleading with him for answers. But I don't hear no reply, do you?'

'Klein I...'

'You back-chattin me, woman?' Klein got to his feet, forgetting the moonshine was nestled in his lap. As he stood, the bottle fell and shattered on the floor. Klein glanced down and watched the only solace in his miserable life spill across the floor. 'You going to pay for that now bitch!'

'Klein, no! I'm sorry, for everything!"

'You get here now, ya hear!'

'Klein no...'

'I said *get*...' He started to take off his belt.

Janet had a choice to make. She wrestled with it as Jacob wrestled with God. She could go into the room and get a beating, or try and make a run for it. Maybe she could wait it out until the moonshine and the rage had dissipated. She could probably get to the Morrisons', but what about the kids? They were asleep upstairs. If they woke and he was in a rage, they would be his punching bag - again.

She weighed it all up. Then made a break for the door. Klein gave chase, the moonshine slowing his movements. But he continued to make up ground on her.

Janet hadn't counted on the front door being locked; she grappled with it, trying to pull it open. It was all in vain; Klein had the key. As Janet turned she could see him bearing down on her. The rest was a blur: fists flying, murder in his eyes, a poker swinging through the air like a hatchet.

She awoke three days later in Juniper Hospital. Klein had been apprehended. It hadn't taken long: he was gloating about his assault to anyone who would listen in his favourite watering hole. Blind drunk, with bloodied fists. They held him on an attempted murder charge. The trial took place another three days later, where he was sentenced to fifteen years.

Janet jumped from her memory as the bell on the oven began to ring. She lifted her head but her split lip had attached itself to her sweater. She managed to pull her face away, but reopened the cut. She licked at it, tasting metallic warmth.

She got up and opened the oven: the smell of roasted feline wafted into the kitchen, reminding her of chicken. She grabbed the oven gloves, took out the carcass and placed it on the side to cool.

A thought crossed her mind, and she idled over to the kitchen cupboard, the one with spices and other consumables. Reaching deep within, she relaxed as she felt the familiar cold leather on her finger-tips. She knew it was safe in there; Klein would never go snooping in the cupboards. The kitchen, to him, was a woman's domain. She gripped the leather spine and pulled out her Bible.

It was battered and well-used; it was the Bible bequeathed to her on her wedding day. Well-worn and thumbed, it had corners held together with tape. She took it back to the table, flicking through it as one might a catalogue. Various passages were highlighted and there were hand-scribbled notes in the margins. Service sheets were half-glued to certain pages. She sat down and placed the Bible in front of her. She knew that good Christians were not supposed to believe in talismans, but having the book there in front of her helped her to focus; she turned her gaze heavenwards.

'Lord, what can I do?'

She leafed through the near translucent pages, returning again to Exodus, one of her favourites. Passage 14:14. She read aloud. Whilst Klein was out, she decided to take the opportunity to read her forbidden text at the top of her voice. It seemed to give the words new meaning as she spoke each one aloud.

'The Lord will fight for you, you need only to be still'. Janet leant back in her chair, a tear filling her eye.

Janet thought about something the Baptist minister had spoken about. Back when there was hope in Juniper, when the town still believed: a time before the flood, the heat and the famine.

Reverend Jacob was a kind man, generous with his time and his flock. He would give much of his meagre wages away to the poor and destitute, and in Juniper there was never a lack of those in need, especially now. As Janet sat there reading the words of her forgotten Lord at the kitchen table, she thought back to the day Reverend Jacob explained an analogy of God's absence.

She was only on her second child back then; feeling deflated, tired, abused and abandoned by both her god and her loving husband.

'Why's life got to be so hard, why doesn't he see me...why doesn't he help?'

'My child, he does see you...'

'Then why doesn't he save me from this...' Janet turned to show a fresh welt to the side of her cheek, a crimson imprint across her cheekbone, spreading up to her eye socket. '...why does this loving God you talk about allow this to happen?'

'My dear, I am sorry...is it happening again? Would you like me to report it this time?'

'No, no, please don't. If you do, he'll kill me, or the kids. He won't be taken away from them...'

'Ok Janet. I won't report it. Please, calm down. Listen, I've a duty of care, a duty of care for you and your children. Think about that. If something were to happen to...'

'It won't, you hear? It won't... If it gets any worse than a few clips every now and again, I'll come to you, I promise.' As Janet mumbled the last two words she instinctively looked away from the Reverend. He was a man of God; if anyone could know she was lying, it would be him.

'OK, Janet, I believe you. As I was saying, don't think that God has abandoned you.'

'Well, it feels like it. Most of the time my prayers go unanswered and I'm at breaking point... I just don't know how much longer I can keep going, what with Klein out all night drin...well, out taking care of business. It's just me here, holding down the house and juggling the babies. When will it end?'

'My child, listen to me. I used to be like you. When I was in training, I wanted everything *now*: gifts of the spirit, prophesy, speaking in tongues... hell, you name it. If it was mentioned in the Bible, I wanted it, and I didn't want to wait...'

'You allowed to say hell?' Janet whispered as to not cause offence.

'Well, you got me there, Janet. Sometimes I do like a cuss word. Been known to say a lot worse in my time, but we've a forgiving God and we're not perfect... I'm sure he'll forgive me the odd hell every now and again.'

'Sorry, I interrupted. Do you mind if I...' Janet pointed down to the baby and her breast. The baby was hungry.

'Of course not, are you OK with me being here while you..?' He pointed between her breast and the baby.

'Sure, you wouldn't be the first person in Juniper to see my breasts. Since you said we've got a forgiving God and all that...take that as my confession if you like!'

'Duly noted.'

Janet unbuttoned her shirt and moved the baby closer to suckle. Janet noticed Reverend Jacob trying to look anywhere other than at her breasts, but she could tell he couldn't help but be drawn to them. His childlike curiosity playing out over his face. Janet mused that it wasn't her breasts that drew his attention, but more the miracle he was witnessing. Janet assumed he'd never seen a mother breast-feeding before; why would he have?

Since he was a child, the Reverend had his heart set on working for the church, in whatever guise that took. He went to Bible college and within his first few months took a vow of celibacy. He wasn't inclined to become a Catholic priest or anything, but he wanted his heart to be on fire for the Lord and no other. No distractions. So, hooking up with women was the last thing on his mind.

He watched Janet coaxing the tiny infant onto her breast. He watched as Janet's nipple grew hard, the small dots around her breast stiffening until it was a peak on a flesh coloured mountain, a milky snow crowning it. She rubbed it teasingly over her child's top lip, back and forth. The child opened its mouth, as a fish would to take bait. She slipped the nipple into its thirsty gummy maw. Janet looked up to find the Reverend staring intently at her, leaning towards her and child, enraptured by the whole process.

'You never seen it before?'

'No, it's fascinating...'

'Yeah, breastfeeding ain't too bad either!'

Both Janet and the Reverend began to chuckle, like two old school friends sharing a joke. Janet stroked her baby's head as she began to suckle. Sometimes she sounded out of breath or even as if she were being smothered, tiny slurps breaking their conversation. The baby's pulsating fontanelle reminded the reverend of John Hurt's chest in that film, *Alien,* right before the horrid critter popped out. It made him feel queasy just looking at it. There was a delicate brain just a few millimetres below that flap of skin where bones were yet to fuse. A stray finger, or an episode of Klein's anger, could pierce it and extinguish that perfect little life with ease.

'Jacob, are you ok?'

'Janet, sorry, I was miles away...what were we discussing?'

'I think you were going to tell me something about how we were similar?'

'Yes...yes, that's it. I was saying that we are alike...in wanting everything now. My teacher at Bible college saw this in me too, the struggles that I had with God, wanting *immediacy*. Feeling as though God had, in some way, distanced himself from me, that my prayers – like yours – were going unanswered, that life was just *happening* to me. It wasn't so much a crisis of faith, more a bump in the road. He sat me down one day and asked me if I'd ever seen a tapestry. Have you ever seen one, Janet?'

'Can't say I have, but I know what they are.'

'That's good! He told me that life is like a tapestry, but that you view it from the back. It doesn't look like much: it's full of knots, frayed pieces of fabric, loose ends. It's ugly, in fact. It's a mishmash of random colours and patterns. But God, he said, views our life from the *other side* of the tapestry. Our threads run through his brilliantly detailed masterpiece. Janet, you have to remember that God sees the complete picture and how your life fits into *his* plan. You may be feeling abandoned and in a pit right now, but in God's tapestry, he has it all planned out and you are one thread that is woven through His work of art. So, take heart, my dear, when you feel burdened and burnt out, alone or in despair. He *does* see you. He *does* know your plight. But, he gave us free will. He doesn't interfere with the design because he can see the masterpiece near its completion.'

As Reverend Jacob finished, he looked up and watched as a tear fell from Janet's face, inching its way down. It wove its way around the red welt, Klein's mark. It ran down the side of her nose, pooling at her philtrum before dripping onto the baby's head. An early baptism, Jacob thought. The tears of a woman cleansing the child of the sins of the father.

'That's probably the most beautiful thing I ever heard, Jacob... You're good...you're real good...too good for this shit hole town, but I might just keep on keeping on!'

'Please, Janet, I beg you, don't give up! It's always darkest before the dawn. Just remember though, that the dawn is coming... If there's nothing else you want to tell me, I'll better be off. Maybe I might see you in church sometime soon?'

'I'll see what I can do. Thank you for tonight, it's been great. You don't mind seeing yourself out, do you? This little one's latched on tighter than a tick on a deer.'

With that, the Reverend left. Janet watched him as he went. She'd known even then that she wouldn't get the chance to go to church; Klein wouldn't allow it. So she sat there, her child suckling at her breast, her daughter's rhythmic swallowing both cathartic and soporific. Her mind wandered to sleep.

Janet was brought back from the reverie by a pain. Twice now she'd been daydreaming, caught up in memory. The pain had brought her out of it, but it was also the pain that drove her into the past. She'd been picking at her arm, the cigarette burn from the night before. A pink, creamy juice ran down her arm; she'd burst the blister.

She plodded across the kitchen, ran her arm under the cold water until it felt numb and the creamy mess had stopped leaking out. She twisted the faucet off, grabbed a small kitchen towel, and wrapped it around her arm, tucking it in tightly until it was securely in place.

The cooked cat was now cooled. She went back to the table, picked up her Bible, and retraced her steps, reaching into the back of the cupboard, placing it in its usual spot. She began rearranging the cupboard with spices and jars, covering it back up, like the Romans rolling the stone across Jesus' tomb. No matter what she put in front of it, no matter the turmeric, coriander, cumin and oregano - there would be no containing her God now. Whether she liked it or not, he'd broken free from the tomb and was jealous for her.

Janet turned to the carcass, an unusual swagger in her step. She picked up a large brown bag and put the whole thing in, tray and all. She rolled down the top of the bag to make a handle for ease of carrying it, then once more caught her reflection in the window.

She was split into many different refractions, different versions of herself. In all of them, Janet noticed her crucifix hanging out again, glinting in the sunlight. She held it for a moment, offered a prayer, then tucked it back inside her jumper.

She knew Klein would give her a good grilling about the window. But she had other, more pressing things to worry about. She marched towards the front door and set off to Betty's.

CHAPTER EIGHT

Betty sat in the library: she was the sole visitor. It could have been due to the heat beginning to wash over the town - but she mused that it was more likely due to this thing called 'the Internet'. She'd heard of it, though never seen it in action. She just knew what computers were, and that this Internet thing lived inside of them, drawing people in to a plastic box full of wondrous delights.

Betty had passed a few people on her way here: walking zombies, hunched over, heads bent, arms rigid, vacant expressions - staring into their mobile phones, never glancing up, obsessed by all the things *they* consumed with their eyes. Betty was old school: didn't miss what she'd never had, and preferred the reliability of books.

She could feel someone approaching, a stirring in the warm air.

'So, these here are what you requested Betty.' Mr. Somerton dropped the books on the table with a thud.

'Thank you, Mr. Somerton. After that walk, I am exhausted... you're far too kind to an old woman like me.'

'Not a problem at all, Betty. It's nice to have someone come in and want to read books, instead of using that infernal contraption over there... It'll make even me, this place, obsolete soon. Mark my words, people won't need books or a silly old man to find them for them, everything will be at the touch of a button.' Mr. Somerton jabbed a finger in the direction of the IT suite in the corner where a solitary computer sat, its screen bright and enticing. 'Most people I've seen the last few weeks have been coming in to use the computer 'cos their Internet's down, power shorted out or something, what with the heat and all... but ours is the same: works half the time, the other half just sits there watching me!'

'That's why I prefer books. They never let you down, do they?'

'Never come across a book that's let me down... except 'Crime and Punishment'. I use it as a doorstop now. Should be burnt, that book, would keep the fire going for hours. But don't you be telling anyone I said that, Betty, I don't want a *Fahrenheit 451*' happening!' Mr. Somerton nudged Betty in a jovial way and added a playful wink. Betty laughed. She didn't know why; his joke was lost on her. She thought he was talking about cooking temperatures, but she just nodded and smiled at him anyway.

'These will do just fine, Mr. Somerton...thank you again for helping me locate them.'

'Your leg playing up again, Betty?'

'N... why do you ask?' Betty was guarded with her response.

'Just all these books about medicine, thought maybe your leg was playing you up is all...'

'Well, it's been awfully stiff these last few days. My back's been aching due to the discrepancy in my leg where they fused it back together. My hip's been sending shooting pains down my leg like someone's scalding me with hot water...' Betty observed Mr. Somerton's eyes wandering away from her. Had he lost interest in the conversation, was she boring him? '...sorry, I do prattle on some, don't I? Don't really have anyone to talk to nowadays since my husband's passing and the children have all flown the coop. Gets lonely some, when you're out on the edge of the town limits.'

'You should get yourself a pet! Cat or something. I could have a word with Janet Lehey see if she got any to spare? Would cost you a pretty penny though, now she's saving the town from the famine with that livestock of hers.'

Betty just nodded.

'Heard her prized – colt, shall we say? Has gone missing: the ginger thing people see roaming around at night...you haven't stolen it, have you?'

'Me... no... I would never...!'

'Woah Betty, calm down, didn't mean anything by it! Was a joke... must be the heat getting to me. Sorry, I didn't mean to insinuate anything. Why don't I just let you get on with what you came here for. Sorry, Betty. I'll be over there if you need me.'

Mr. Somerton retreated like a scolded schoolboy, his shoulders slumped forward as he shuffled back to his desk near the front of the library. Betty thought about consoling him, telling him that she meant nothing by it, but thought it best to let it slide, in case she let something slip.

Betty began searching through the jaunty tower of hardback books on the table. She'd kept it vague when requesting them, so as not to give away anything. The first detailed how to splint fractured and broken legs, both human and livestock – livestock being cows and horses, not the new meaning the town had come to prefer.

Betty scribbled some notes down on a piece of paper, items that she might need to acquire from the convenience store a few doors down. Her list consisted of bandages, pain killers, tape and splints. She placed the book to one side, slowly working her way through the stack and building a more solid structure of those she had read or disregarded on the other side of the desk.

The next book was old and dusty, the cover marked with a yellowy stain. When Betty opened it, a dank smell struck her nostrils: mildew – it was comforting, in a sad way.

Betty began flicking through the pages. The book was published in 1947, and filled with graphic images. It brimmed with in-depth photographs and articles about reconstructive surgeries performed on veterans returning from the Second World War.

Broken and torn bodies littered the pages, as their severed limbs and mangled body parts did the battlefields.

Stumps and holes.

Cuts and tears.

Shrapnel and maiming – all exposed and in gory detail.

She found the section she was after: Facial Deformities. Tom's injuries surfaced in her mind's eye. The poor creature was horribly disfigured. The picture staring back at her from the book's pages could have been of Tom, only clean shaven. The jaw hung loose and corrupted; small, broken, black stubs of teeth glinting out of a mushy pit where a mouth should have been.

Betty remembered when Maggie had stood on a glass bauble at Christmas, shattering it. Glistening fragments of white glass poked out of the sole of her foot. Betty spent hours fighting the bloody spillage, slippery hands searching the glistening wound, removing one luminous shard after another.

Betty continued to flick through the book until she found the section on lower face injuries. Some of the photos showed pre-and post-surgery, whereas others were reduced to gruesome images adorned with brief footnotes, indicating the patient didn't make it through. But they were still cataloged, for reasons Betty could only guess at. Frozen in time, honoured by having their mangled bodies and faces displayed for the world to see – not who they were, but the grotesqueries that they had become.

Many of those detailed had their lower jaw completely removed, leaving an open wound with a fatty, swollen tongue lolling in the dark hole of their throat, a top row of teeth like stalactites hanging down from the roof of a cave.

It seemed from the footnotes that the majority of these nameless faces died due to complications resulting from the surgery and the infections that ensued. There were also details about pioneering surgeries, often in response to ghastly wounds the doctors had never come across previously. Betty saw it was more like guesswork than anything else: nutty professor stuff, carte blanche for those surgeons to try whatever they felt like, to see if some of it worked.

Many of the soldiers that did survive were left abominations, with scars and deformities that would haunt them for the rest of their lives. Death would have been kinder. Death wouldn't have mocked or ridiculed them. Death would not have turned them into something they never wished to be. Death would have been finite and peaceful.

This search was proving fruitless for her, so Betty decided to move onwards; the jaw would have to be something she addressed later.

She felt a trickle of sweat on the back of her neck. Her mouth was dry. She wondered if people without lower-jaws experienced dry mouth, or was it just a constant throb of agony without relief? The building was heating up as the sun's glow magnified to radioactive levels. She thought of bombs, and then tried not to think about them.

She'd moved seats a few times already, trying to get further away from the beams of light streaking through the windows. She wondered whether, if the heat got too much, the building would become a tinder box, and all these books fuel for the fire: all this history, all this information, here today and gone tomorrow.

But the books seemed to not fall in the direct path of the window light, and on inspecting the floor she could see that the bookcases had been moved out of the sun's glare. The floorboards were darker where the cases used to stand.

Mr. Somerton was busy fanning himself with a pamphlet from the Baptist Church bake sale. Betty laughed as she watched him. '*Bake sale*' she muttered to herself. 'The only thing baking is us!' She stood, clutching books.

'I'll help you with that, Betty! You don't have to put them back.'

'It's okay, Mr. Somerton. I need to get up and walk around a bit...' She hit her hip '...need to keep this thing moving before it stiffens up, be murder on the way back home if I've not put it through its paces.'

'Well, if you're sure.'

'Please, it would be my pleasure.'

Mr. Somerton returned to his fanning, stopping every now and again to systematically re-organise the piles of books littered on his desk.

He must be desperate for something to do, Betty mused.

The thud, thud, thud of the books was soothing and rhythmic, like a faint heartbeat clinging to life.

Betty was pleased that she'd been able to move out of the presence of Mr. Somerton, as she had one last book she wanted to look up, but didn't want to draw attention to her secret quest. She hobbled down the medical history aisle, letting her fingers dance across the spines of the books. She stopped when she located a gap, chances were it belonged to one of the books she had in her hands. If not, it would be one of the other hardbacks on the table that she would come back and return later.

After repeating this dance a couple of times, she'd replaced all the books on the shelves. Betty peered through the bookcases, noticing Mr. Somerton still seated at the desk and hearing the faint thud, thud of his work. She knew she was free to locate what she was looking for, away from any prying eyes.

She found the book fairly quickly and returned to another desk, the one furthest from Mr. Somerton, in the back of the library where all the books and pamphlets about the town were stored. It was in the dark, as she approached the desk, she felt a sudden coldness; a chill that had long vanished from Juniper even in its winter months. It was eerie but somewhat enticing, sensual even. Her arms prickled with goosebumps as she pulled out the seat, placing the book on the table. She pulled the chain on the green table lamp.

The bulb ignited after flickering intermittently for a few seconds. Sitting down, she flicked through the pages until she found the right chapter.

Castration.

She'd already seen that Tom was in heat, the pearlescent baby gravy he'd spilled last night highlighting that she needed, at some point, to remove these urges. Although deep down she knew it wasn't a case of *need*, it was selfishness that made her want to do it. Betty wanted to keep him close and a new constant in her life. Castration was meant to stop creatures from roaming, and she couldn't bear the thought of that, of someone leaving her alone again. She thought that whilst he was bed ridden due to his injuries would be the best time to perform such an act. His limited mobility would help his recovery, in the end. He wouldn't be leaping about, scratching and pulling out stitches.

Betty scanned the document in front of her, astounded by the various options at her disposal. There was something called banding – where you place a tight band above each teste, cutting off the blood supply, which eventually caused the organs to shrivel up and drop off, the body taking care of the rest.

But it appeared quite time-consuming, and also required a special stretching tool to fit the bands. All she had at her disposal were elastic bands, and they wouldn't cut the mustard. Where was she going to get one of those stretching tools, without drawing unwanted attention? She rubbished the idea.

There were other ways of performing a castration; some involving slicing the testes, pulling out the kidney bean-shaped sack, pulling it tightly to ensure you had got enough of the tube to work with, before twisting, knotting and cutting it off. The images showed how to tie the right knots, aided by arrows showing the direction of flow and pull. Even though she didn't have testicles, seeing this made her feel queasy; brought a sinking sympathetic feeling to the pit of her stomach.

Betty laid the book down, glanced up to see where Mr. Somerton was as she came out in a cold sweat. The steady thud, thud had stopped. He was now placing the books in a library trolley, soon to start his rounds of returning their books to their various nooks and crannies. She hastily scribbled notes, including diagrams of the knots she'd need to perform, and added a few more entries to her shopping list. Razors. A scalpel or something to cut with. Something to wash the wound. And diapers.

Mr. Somerton pushed the library cart down one aisle; then as if by magic he appeared the next aisle along. The wheel at the front of the trolley was a little wonky and made the whole thing do a shuddering dance as Mr. Somerton pushed the cart through the library. Every now and then, he stopped to place a book back. Betty folded her notes and stuffed them into her pocket.

'Making some notes are we, Betty? That will be $5...'

'Oh...this...' She pulled the piece of paper back from her pocket and waved it in the air '...it's just my shopping list.'

'It was a joke, Betty.'

'Oh right. Well I guess the heat's getting to me, sorry Mr. Somerton.'

Betty got up from the table, using it to pull herself into a standing position. She'd been sitting far too long and her hip had frozen in place. After a few small stretches, using the table as leverage, she managed to bring the old thing back into life.

Betty began to push the chair back under the desk, when she noticed the book was still on the table. She quickly picked it up and began to walk toward Mr. Somerton. She could tell he had his eyes on the book, but her arms were covering the title. As she wobbled closer, she began to panic. *What if he asks about the title?* she thought. Her mind came alive with excuses, things to say if questioned, drawn out explanations as to why she was reading that particular book.

'Betty, may I ask...'

Here it comes, she thought. Betty could feel her face reddening

'...why do you insist on calling me "Mr. Somerton?" You know my name is Richard.'

As she approached the trolley, she pretended to stumble over the front wheel, tipping the cart and the books onto the ground; they fell like dying butterflies, pages flapping like wings, until they hit the floor.

'Oh, I am so sorry Mr. Somerton – I mean Richard! Do forgive this daft old lady! Here, let me...'

'No, no, Betty, it's quite all right. I'll have all these picked up in no time.' Richard bent down and began to collect the scattered books. Betty took this as her only shot. She quickly placed the book on the trolley, stuffing it between a couple of other books roughly the same size and shape.

'So, why *do* you always call me "Mr. Somerton"?'

The voice scared her. She turned inch by inch, expecting to see accusing eyes staring back at her, but she was relieved to find that his eyes were turned downward to the fallen books. He picked each one up like an entomologist might their specimens, wondering what had happened to them.

'I guess it's just something that stuck. You've been in this town longer than most and, well, you were working here when I was still a young girl. I've always known you as Mr. Somerton... Guess my parents taught me manners, and they're a hard thing to come by in Juniper. You should be flattered! I could be calling you Dick.' They both began to chuckle.

'Right you are, Betty, right you are. Haven't been called Dick in a long time. It's just, when you call me Mr. Somerton... I don't know, makes me just feel that little bit older. But hey, that's my name isn't it? Can't be changing it now. You call me Mr Somerton if you want, dear.' He stood up, stretching his back, and placing the books back on the trolley.

'Well, I best be off, got some more errands to run before the long walk home. Pleasure seeing you again Mr – sorry, force of habit – Richard.' Betty began walking to the table where she left her stick.

'No problem at all. You're welcome anytime, maybe see you around?'

'I don't come into town as much as I like.'

Stick in hand, she headed for the door, walking through the beams of light slicing through the window, causing her skin to break out in sweat with just a brush.

'Well, maybe you pay some thought to what I said, ya hear?' Betty turned to face Richard.

'What was that?'

"Bout you getting a cat.'

She went specifically to the checkout with a young girl manning the till. She figured they would most probably find an elderly woman purchasing diapers horrific rather than interesting, so she paid and crumpled the brown paper bag under her free arm and hobbled out away from Marge Supplies.

She laughed as she left the supply store; what with it being called Marge Supplies, you'd expect it to have actual items of need. But the shelves were bare, and most of the things for sale were second hand or partly used – though Betty had been in luck and managed to get everything she needed. She'd had to pay over the odds to get the diapers, but they were a luxury item, no doubt. The pack had been opened and there were only half left in there – but they'd have to do.

As she walked, her stick clicked on the sidewalk, setting a steady pace to her march. The town was empty, barring shadows. The sun shone from its zenith, the highest point of the day, so the shadows sulked underneath their casters. She hadn't anticipated being out this long. Her investigations in Juniper Library had taken up far too much time already, delayed by Mr. Somerton's incessant conversation.

She paused outside a boarded-up tourist office and leant her stick up against the wood covering the cracked and dirty panes. She shifted the brown bag under her arm, the crumpling paper loud in the stillness, then glanced about to check that she wasn't drawing any unwanted attention. Adjusted her shawl as best she could, creating a makeshift hood.

She could feel the sweat weighing down her sparse hair, errant droplets snaking into small rivers at the back of her nape, then wending down her spine. Her back sodden already.

Once happy that she was amply covered and not at risk of burning in the unbearable heat, she took back hold of her stick and continued to march, as best she could with her gammy leg, towards the 701.

She passed a number of buildings on the outskirts of town; little houses with windows secured to keep the heat out. She could hear the gentle humming of air conditioning units working in overdrive. She stole glances at the occupants as she walked past their windows: sipping ice-cold water, wearing sweaters in their air-conditioned abodes.

She cursed them under her breath. What a difference electricity would make, if she could afford it; but as her father used to say '*You can't miss something you never had*'. She smiled to herself and continued on. To distract herself from the heat and the pain, she focused on her new project of *fixing* the mangled ginger tom – in more ways than one.

One of the last buildings she passed on the way to the 701 was the Juniper PD, a structure that was as practical as it was ugly. Each cell was marked with a single, tiny, dulled-glass window, no more than a couple of inches wide and about two feet tall. There were far too many for such a small town, she thought.

The glass slits in the wall reminded Betty of arrow niches, the type found on castle walls in England that she'd seen in books as a child. The rest of the building was solid, red-brick, a foreboding eyesore. Razor wire covered the roof like a ghastly halo.

When Betty was younger, she'd visited Northern Ireland; this was during the troubles. It had cost a pretty penny. But with the money they saved on not having the comforts of others, and the selling of some farmland, they set out on this once in a lifetime trip – her parents insisting on reminding her at every opportunity how *much* it had cost them. The intended purpose of said trip was to visit family who'd relocated for a better life. How wrong they were. She'd noticed that the police stations there were fortified, as if to withstand an army, and Juniper PD was the same: a fortress. But for a town of this size, with drunk and disorderly the police's bread and butter, she couldn't help but think it was a little over the top.

Were Juniper law enforcement going for intimidation, or did they know something that the rest of the town didn't? Had 9/11 put the shits up every law enforcement service in America, or was it a deterrent for any criminal activity? Was it a backup for the Juniper Correctional Facility? She hadn't a clue; there were too many questions and not enough hours in the day.

She passed the main entrance, negotiating the thick-fingered bollards protruding from the ground to stop any car intent on ramming the station.

There she stopped dead in her tracks. The town noticeboard at front of the building had a few new bulletins since her last foray into town, which drew her attention.

There was an advert from Janet Lehey: 'Janet's Livestock - all you need to survive!'. Janet was taking orders in the same way people did for Thanksgiving turkeys. There were tickets pre-cut and perforated at the bottom, Janet's address and number printed on tear-away strips that could be ripped off and taken home to deal with in the shade. There were only two of the strips left now.

'*Business must be booming*', Betty mused. She took a slip, though for what reason she didn't know. Looking back at her handiwork, she saw that the last slip dangling beneath the poster resembled a single child's tooth in an otherwise toothless gummy mouth.

There were other bulletins: warnings and health recommendations from the police regarding the floods and now the heat. How to keep safe and hydrated, what to do in an emergency; messages urging the townsfolk to be on the lookout for members of the community they hadn't seen for a while. *'What a load of horse shit!'*, Betty muttered to herself, her thoughts turning to the absence of visitors to her place since the heat struck. Did anyone care? Did they think she was dead already, out on her farm – shrivelled up like a prune by the heat?

There were other warnings too: warnings to stay vigilant about drifters coming into town. What any drifters might want in this Godforsaken town was anyone's guess. The locals were told to lock their doors in the evenings. There were signs about sightings of strange wild cats. Brandenburg had put up a sign warning about keeping valuable livestock inside, since he'd lost one of his to a beast of the night.

Betty knew, like the rest of the town, that this was due to the over-breeding at Lehey's, but no one dared point the finger at the only resource that was keeping the town fed. Well, at least that would remain true until the inbred, deranged cats inevitably killed a human child. Then the mob would act as one and lynch the Lehey's.

It occurred to Betty that when they ran out of food, people might start turning their hunger pains onto their neighbour.

There were a few wanted and missing persons posters covering the remainder of the board. Many of them were old and faded. There was something about one of them that kept her attention. It was newer than the rest, the paper yet to fade or curl.

Robert Black *5ft 10. Medium build. Fair-skinned. Brown eyes.*

Identifying marks: *Faded tattoo of snake on right arm. Tattoo of
the Confederate flag on left hand.
Scar to right side of face from lip to eye.*

Wanted for attempted murder. *If you have any information* *regarding his whereabouts please contact your Local Law Enforcement. Do not approach as highly dangerous.*

Please quote the reference 345890.

There was a picture of Robert Black. He looked strangely familiar to Betty – something about the eyes. A frisson of recognition stole across her mind, like déjà vu but foggier, perhaps due to the heat.

Betty hoped that something in her rapidly dehydrating brain would fall into place as she stared intently at the poster. Where had she seen those eyes? It was a recent encounter, but for the life of her she couldn't get the grey matter to work.

She blew a droplet of sweat away that had collected at the tip of her nose and watched as it arced through the air and landed on the glass casing of the notice board. Betty could have sworn it hissed as it struck. She became engrossed as it began to evaporate almost immediately.

The eyes plagued her: there was something familiar about them, something uncanny. Where had she seen them? She'd thought she would have placed the scar straightaway: facial deformities gave her the creeps, and bad oral hygiene was worse. Did that make her a snob? Quite possibly. She wracked her brain. Had it been a fleeting encounter? Someone she bumped in to? Her mind turned to the convicts on her way into Juniper, the ones knelt down in the dirt, maybe it had been one of those men?

Maybe the poster was older than she thought. Perhaps they had already apprehended this individual and he was doing time for his crimes. However much she tried to claw back the fleeting glances she had of those convicts, their profiles, the placement of that particular face eluded her.

Those eyes! Deep, brown, chocolate puddles, so dark the iris and pupil were one. She turned begrudgingly from the notice board, wrestling with her mind, and continued the long, hot walk. Her stick clacked once more on the pavement with each wobble of her weary legs. The paper bag rustling under her arm, she waddled towards home as a penguin might after a long quest for food. Different climates but an arduous journey nevertheless, and neither with a guarantee of safe return.

CHAPTER TEN

Janet had been killing time at Betty's house. She'd tried the door, pulled the screen back on its squeaking hinges, knocked a good number of times, but there was no answer.

She'd peered in through the front room window, the net curtains were dusty and dirty and obscured most of her view, but from what she could tell there was no sign of life. Janet placed the feline offering on the steps leading up to the house and sat down next to it, the wood groaned under her weight.

Janet concealed herself within the shade offered by the overhanging and dilapidated porch, musing to herself that she could ask Klein to come over and fix it. She soon rubbished the thought when she brushed a rogue spindle of hair from her face and her fingers touched the bruise from last night's encounter. She didn't want to suffer another so soon. Asking Klein to do anything he didn't want to do inevitably contributed to her growing collection of bruises.

The sun stole in through the holes in the porch, bright and straight like stakes of light. Janet reached out a hand, left it dancing in the beam, but it soon became unbearable and she withdrew it, licking the spot where it had been burned.

It reminded her of her daughter, Mia, who once singed Janet with a magnifying glass, using it to harness the full force of the sun. It was summer, and Janet was sitting in the chair-swing in the garden. Mia was busying herself around her mother's feet, using the magnifying glass Klein had given her to burn up leaves and explode ants. It wasn't long before Mia decided to direct the pinprick of light onto her mother's foot. As Mia got the rays to converge, Janet screamed with pain.

It was the same sort of pain she had now, white and bright. Janet watched as a car sped past Betty's, down the 701 toward Juniper. Dust flew into the sky in its wake. She mused it was best they kept on going: there was nothing left in this town other than failed ambition and scorched earth.

Janet heard something, a low guttural sound coming from the house. It had crept up on her, a noise she was unsure she was really hearing; working in the background, building to the crescendo that now drew her attention. It sounded as if something was in pain. She stood, her buttocks leaving a damp patch from where she had been sitting - the sweat. Janet hoped that she wasn't left with an embarrassing wet patch.

She wiped her sweaty hands on her top and headed back up the rickety steps to the front door. She twisted the handle, wondering why she hadn't tried it previously. The place was locked up tight. The noise was louder, though still muffled, something in pain but unable to cry out. Janet wondered if it was Betty. Had she fallen over? Was she unable to get up? What if the noise she was hearing was Betty's last words?

The thought filled her with horrified adrenaline. Janet scampered around the farmstead, dancing in and out of the beams of light tumbling in from loose tiles and the ruptured roof which framed three sides of the property. The wood creaked under her footing as she moved around to the kitchen side of the house. She made her hand into a fist and began rubbing the grime from the window, peering in through the cleared pane.

Janet still couldn't see anything untoward, just a lot of mess: plates with half-eaten food on the floor near the sofa, the sink full of soiled plates, photos strewn across the wall haphazardly. Sweat trickled down her brow, stinging her eyes, irritating the various cuts and abrasions on her face. She dabbed at the blemishes with the sleeve of her top.

Something moved in the house. Janet pressed her face up to the glass, her forehead resting on grime, eyes peering into the cluttered abode. She could have sworn she saw something move within. Something low and hunched.

She waited in silence, like a barn owl hovering in the sky waiting to be alerted to a tasty morsel foraging in the undergrowth. Whatever it was that had moved did not stir again. The sound she originally heard seemed to have gone too. Was it her dehydrated mind playing tricks on her?

Janet snaked her way back around the porch to the steps at the front door, sitting down on the wood she had soiled with her sweat. It was now bone dry, much like her throat. Exertion in this heat was almost a death sentence. Janet was already tired and weary. Her eyelids grew heavy, each blink longer than the last, until darkness took her over.

CHAPTER ELEVEN

'Hello...'

Betty hobbled towards home, small tendrils of steam – or was it smoke – hovering over the long, yellow grass. She mused over the possibility of another bush fire, the whole of Juniper waiting for a shard from a broken bottle or a discarded cigarette to set the place ablaze.

'Hello...eh... Betty?'

Betty turned, trying to figure out where the noise was coming from, it was insistent, like an annoying wasp. It was Andrea Thomas, sat underneath the shade of her porch. Betty must have passed her without noticing and now stopped in her tracks. The sun beating down upon her seemed to intensify whilst she was stationary.

'Oh...it is you!' Andrea said. 'What are you doing out in this heat?

Betty lifted her bag.

'I had to run a few errands...' Betty turned to walk away, unwilling to stay still for too long. She needed to get home, needed to drink some water, and find the comforting shade of her house. But most importantly, she needed to get back to Tom.

'You should have stopped by on your way, Betty. I'm sure John would have run you into town. He headed that way himself not too long ago, to get some provisions. Not long now, you know...' Andrea placed a hand on her stomach, turned to the side to show Betty how far along she was. '...the doctor says it could be any day.'

Betty stared at the bloated woman before her: her face was red as a tomato, sweat dripping off her as she stood in what looked like a bedsheet. Swollen hands, feet, and ankles - so swollen that the skin could pop at any moment.

'Nothing good can come of this...' Betty murmured.

'What's that, Betty? I can't quite hear you! Why don't you come on over and rest in the shade for a while?'

'Can't!' Betty hollered back 'Food's gunna spoil if I don't get it back soon. You take care now!' With that, she was back on the road. She didn't wait for a response from Andrea.

Betty heard the screen door slam shut behind her, meaning Andrea had gone back inside to slow-cook her child.

'Nothing good can come of it – bringing a child into this place, this mess. It will be overcooked and under fed...' Betty talked to herself '...an abomination, putting yourself through all that. The strain, the poverty of it all. That child, if it survives, will be struggling from day one. This heat is going to cook up something crazy in there.'

As she neared home, she began to think about the soldiers she'd seen in the books from the library, the horrific images coming to her in flashes. The heat continued to bear down on her and she could feel herself getting weaker, but home was on the horizon. With each shuffling step it drew that much closer, so she continued.

Flash after gory flash hit her, with each step something more graphic dropped into her mind, as if someone were dropping slides into a projector.

Severed limbs.

Shrapnel injuries.

Grenade survivors.

Twisted, broken bodies.

Betty licked at her dry lips, the skin cracked and sore, the cracks feeling like deep ravines. Charred bodies, skin blackened and split open. Eyes splayed across the face like fried eggs. Popped in the heat of the blaze and cooked over the chargrilled flesh. Limbs shrivelled and pulled in tight, like dead spiders. She remembered something, a phrase from a story she'd read, long ago now but it came back to her like she was reading it afresh, and so began muttering it aloud to herself, partly to keep her brain occupied and to ensure she didn't collapse and become one of her charred visions – the opening paragraph to 'Metamorphosis' by David Eagleman.

'There are three deaths...' she said. 'The first is when the body ceases to function.' Her own body seemed to be shutting down, as she trampled the last leg of her journey, each step as if she were walking through a muddy bog. 'The second is when the body is consigned to the grave.' At this, an image of Normandy Cemetery hit, coming to mind with such ferocity it almost knocked her off her weakened feet: she remembered the white crosses and stars in stark contrast to the green grass, bodies of thousands of Americans all consigned to the grave on foreign soil. 'The third is that moment, sometime in the future, when your name is spoken for the last time.'

Betty experienced a vision of herself, passed out on the side of the road. Fire swirled around her, catching hold of her clothes and then consuming her flesh, corrupting her body and turning it to ash. A sharp breeze blew what remained of her body away, ash ascending into the sky, scattering her across the dusty inferno that was Juniper.

Would she even be missed? Was her brief encounter with Andrea actually the third death? She was sure her children never spoke of her anymore; never called, wrote or visited. Why would they? There was nothing here for them, just a shell of a house, a wreck of a town, and a lost mother. Her husband was dead, consigned to the grave; Betty was just surviving and perhaps in that sense she was already dead, because she had lost her purpose.

The sound of something moving suddenly in the dead grass beside her woke Betty from the conscious nightmare. Dazed from the vision's intensity, she stumbled, planting her stick in the ground to stop herself from falling. She took a moment to shake the ghosts from her head. She'd made it; she was home.

She stood at the end of the driveway leading to her farmstead.

Almost there, you can do it...

She turned off the 701, following the gravel path leading up to her house, the ground crunching under each well-placed foot. Spiders scurried from the stones, hopping over the gravel. Small carcasses of what she presumed were mice lay desiccated and burned up, skin all taut and papery.

She glanced out into the field, wondering if Janet's livestock had something to do with it. She scanned the bushes, waiting to see beady eyes staring back at her, willing her to fall, succumb to the heat, pass out and become a free meal. She continued to scan through the withered plants as she shuffled up to her farm house porch.

A few steps away – that was when she saw her lying there, passed out on her front steps. Janet.

Betty's heart began to race, pounding heavy and hard against her chest. She could almost feel it rattling her ribcage. A frisson of fear and dread washed over her, cooling her skin. She felt an odd sensation that she'd not felt for a long time; it hurt for a brief moment as her flesh broke out in goosebumps.

Had Janet discovered her secret? Was Janet here to out her as having done the unthinkable? What would the townsfolk say when they found out what she had done, what she was capable of?

Betty pushed these thoughts to the back of her jumbled and busy mind, hobbling towards the stricken woman. As Betty got closer to Janet, her eyes turned from the forlorn body on the ground and began roving the grounds of her home. The screen door was open and ajar, but the main door was still locked – Janet had been prying, it would seem. The windows all seemed secured. No forced entry.

Betty stepped over Janet, noticing her chest still rising and falling, breathing laboured but still rhythmic. A wave of anxiety left her body.

There wasn't a car in the driveway; Janet must have walked here, but she wasn't dressed for the heat. Stupid woman must have passed out with heat exhaustion, the exertion of walking all this way, Betty thought. Though it touched her someone had come all this way to see her.

Betty placed her shopping on the porch swing, the rusted chains creaking for a moment before they resumed their redundancy: Betty couldn't remember the last time she took to the swing.

Taking one last peek at Janet, she moved around the side of the house, leaving her stick leaning on the porch balustrade, so she'd make less noise. As she shuffled around the porch, Betty checked the windows.

'All seems secure,' she mumbled. 'But what was this?'

Betty noticed that the kitchen window looked clean, as though someone had wiped it down to get a look inside.

Betty pressed her nose against the pane of glass, her hands shaking as she shielded her eyes from the light and peered in. Nothing.

Then, she saw a bloody trail leading from the lounge toward the front door. 'Shit.'

Betty shuffled back through the dappled light seeping through her broken roof, toward the front door. Janet was still unconscious. Picking up her shopping, Betty rummaged in her pocket for the key. Gingerly, she placed the key in the door handle and twisted.

It was stuck. The door hit something hidden, something heavy blocking its path. She pressed against the door with all her might. She was exhausted, but fear allowed her to muster enough strength to shift the weight of the hidden blockage. There was a low thud as the concealed mass hit the floorboards. Betty crept inside, checking as she did so that Janet was still unawares.

'What did you do?' Betty whispered.

The ginger tom stared at her, vacant eyes in a broken bloody face.

'Right, let's get you somewhere safe... Mamma's going to take care of you soon enough.'

CHAPTER TWELVE

'What the hell?' Janet said, as she came around. Iciness moved across her skin, a shock like one of Klein's slaps. Janet tried to get up but slipped on the steps. Glancing up, to see Betty standing above her with an empty chamber pot.

'You passed out, my love. Only thing I could think of to get you awake and cool you down. Heat exhaustion, I think?' Janet noticed a small smirk on Betty's face.

'Well, I guess I owe you some type of thank you?'

'No bother...is that for me?'

'Is what for you?'

'That there? In the brown bag.'

Janet picks up the bag on the step. The paper crinkled in one hand, she stood, supporting herself on the balustrade.

'Yeah, I brought you a little something. Klein said he saw you on the road the other day, collecting road kill. I just couldn't sit at home thinking of you out here...'

'Ooh, can I see?' Betty put out her hands, itching to see what Janet had brought.

'It's one of mine.' Janet handed over the bag '...it's one of the big ones so should see you good for a few days. How's things out here? I wasn't snooping but if you need some help with fixing the place up...' Janet pointed to the holes in the porch roof, 'I can see if Klein might be able to, or knows someone that can come fix these for you?'

'No bother. It's not like it's raining!' Betty opened the bag and looked inside. As the smell of freshly cooked meat escaped, her mouth instantly began to water.

'What's cat taste like? I've been finding my fair share of roadkill but never turned up any feline to date!' Betty offered, as she hunkered over the open bag, inhaling the rich aroma, dribble escaping her mouth and dripping into the bag.

'It's an acquired taste, the meat's kind of hard, whatever way you cook it. Best way I've found to prepare it is by roasting it, have it cook in its own meagre fluids. That way it's a bit like beef jerky, but with gamey notes. Keeps for ages too, some say it's quite like pheasant but chewier – sorry I'm rambling, I'm sure it will see you good, just don't mention that it was one of the larger ones.' At this Janet tapped the side of her nose and gave a comical wink.

'Well, thank you, Janet... best be off, hadn't you?' Betty's tone was abrupt and distant, but also leaking anxiety.

'Er... well... I guess so.'

'No time like the pheasant... sorry, present, is there? You don't want Klein wondering where you got to, do you?' Janet felt that Betty wanted to say something else but was showing some form of restraint.

'No, you're right. Would you mind if I came inside to get a drink? I'm so thirsty... don't want you finding me out there on one of your harvesting missions!' Janet laughed.

Betty was stone-faced, weighing up her options.

'I guess that would be okay, but you'll need to be quick as I've got a lot to do before the sun goes down. Come on in.'

'Thank you Betty, you're a lifesaver...'

'More than you know, dear...' Betty headed inside. The screen door slammed behind her. Janet dusted herself off and followed after her. The floorboards were already drying, steam rising from the damp boards left by the spillage.

Janet reached for the screen door; it creaked with her pulling.

'Wipe your feet!' Betty called from the darkness of the house.

Janet wandered inside, expecting the place to be a mess, but taken aback by the cleanliness. She entered the kitchen to find Betty hunched over the sink. The plates and detritus she'd glimpsed through the window were gone. The place was spotless. She took a peep in the lounge: the plates were tidied, mess cleared away.

'How long was I passed out for, Betty?'

'Don't know, love. I woke you just as soon as I got back... came in here to get the water to throw over you. The rest is history, as they say.'

Janet held her tongue.

'You feeling okay?' Betty asked, simpering.

'Yes. It's just, I told Klein I wouldn't be long is all. You know what he can be like with....' Janet stopped herself, though she suspected from Betty's earlier remarks she knew enough. '...what were you doing in town?'

'Oh...I had some errands to run. Had to stop off and see Mr. Somerton too, you know, at the library.' Betty turned the faucet on, left it running for a bit. She placed a finger underneath the stream of water, waiting for it to get cold. It didn't. Betty filled the glass up with tepid water instead, shutting the faucet off and turning to Janet, who was looking around her house with what Betty concluded was slightly too close attention.

'You looking for something, Janet?' Betty crossed the kitchen with the glass outstretched.

'Oh... no... I just thought I heard something. Something moving around in here?'

'It's just me here, roaming around in this oversized coffin...come sit.' Betty tried to lead Janet back into the kitchen. She pulled a chair out and waved Janet over to it. Janet took the proffered cup from Betty's hand.

'Thank you, Betty....' Janet gulped the water. Her stomach rumbled with the sudden influx. 'Wow, didn't realise how thirsty I was.'

'You've already lost.' Betty offered with a sigh.

'What do you mean?'

'When you realise you're thirsty, you've already lost the battle. It means you're already dehydrated. You've got to keep up the fluid intake throughout the day. You feeling thirsty is your brain's way of saying it's already suffering from dehydration.'

'Wow, I never knew that. Where you learn that from?'

'Oh, I think it was in a book I read once. At the library...' Betty noticed Janet picking at her arm, where the burn mark was. Betty knew what it was, and how it was caused. 'How'd you get that? Looks nasty.' She nodded toward Janet's arm.

Janet glanced down at her fingers, roving over the burn mark 'Oh... this. I did it when I was cooking the other night, burnt it on a pan.' Her face reddened with the lie. She moved her hand from the blister and tucked it beneath her leg to stop it finding its way back there.

'You got cigarette shaped pans now, have you?'

'I don't know what you mean?'

'That there, it's a cigarette burn...'

'No, this was...'

'So what about that...' Betty pointed at Janet's face, her index finger swirling in a circle, ensuring she covered all the blemishes and cuts.

'I fell...'

'What, you fell after the cigarette shaped pan burnt you? What you land on? A fist shaped table?'

'Betty, I don't appreciate you making assertions about things you have no idea about. What happens...' Janet's voice was shrill. It wavered, as if about to shatter.

Betty reached out a hand, touched the flesh of Janet's arm, a gesture of reassurance. Janet stopped abruptly, looking down at

Betty's hand on her arm, the fingers finding one of the few places without blemish or scar.

Betty felt a sudden flush of sadness for the beaten woman before her 'It's okay Janet... I know we haven't seen eye to eye before and you don't really know me all too well. You probably think I'm some dotty old cow, living all the way out here like some witch. But I know what it's like. I've been where you are.' Betty looked at Janet. To Janet, looking at Betty was like looking at her own mother, a face she'd almost forgotten. 'It's not easy. I don't think I have any answers, but I have two ears and lots of time...'

'Did your... husband...'

'No, no, Jed would never lay a hand on me...' Betty relinquished Janet's arm, began picking a nail on her other hand.

'It was my father, that cantankerous son-of-a-bitch...' Betty reached down and unbuttoned her cuff while Janet watched in mute anticipation. Betty turned up her cuff and then slowly slid the sleeve of her top up. Janet saw the full extent of what Betty was speaking of. Raised welts of scar-tissue covered her arms in a sleeve of puckered flesh. They were too numerous to count. Burned flesh melted into more flesh, each pockmark like a dead fish eye stuck to her flesh.

'Stop, Betty, please...' Janet's voice wobbled and Betty realised that she'd shown too much. She pulled the sleeve back down, hiding the horrors of the past.

'I'm sorry...' Betty reached out again to comfort Janet. Janet flinched.

'I've got to go, Betty. I can't... I just need to go...' Janet pushed her chair back and stood, flustered and confused. Her fingers returned to the burn and she began picking at it again furiously. Betty stood and ambled toward the door. Janet followed, like a little beaten puppy. Betty limped outside, holding open the screen door.

'Janet, you know where I am if you need anything...'

Janet was still picking at her arm as she skulked past Betty. She paused on the threshold, as though weighing a decision. Then, she turned to face Betty and lunged for her.

Betty took a wobbling step back, preparing herself for impact, an altercation she was always going to lose, given her age and dodgy leg.

Janet wrapped her arms around Betty and the older woman realised she had misjudged: the feral act was actually an embrace. Betty let her do it. Gently, she placed a hand on Janet's back, pulling Janet closer like a mother to a child.

The tears poured from Janet's eyes as blood would gush from a mortal wound, a never-ending tide of sadness. Her body fidgeted uncontrollably within Betty's arms, as if she had chronic Parkinson's, deep guttural sounds tumbled from her mouth with each wracking heave. Betty felt the cold tears roll down her cheek and then her neck.

'It's okay... It's okay love...' Betty peeled Janet from her. '...as I said, when you are ready, I'll be here.'

Janet wiped her nose on her sleeve, brushed herself down, and then stood up straight. She walked over to the steps and began to descend. Betty waddled back to the door, turned, watched Janet leave.

'I'll be by next week, Betty...' Janet called over her shoulder. '...to pick up the dish, check if you need anything else...'

'Don't get many visitors out this way, so the company would be welcome...you get now!' Betty shooed her away as someone would a pesky cat.

'Maybe we can talk some more?' Janet's feet crunched onto the gravel.

'I'd like that.'

'Could you do me a small favour?' She turned to look back at Betty.

'Yeah, sure. What you after?'

'Just, if you see Bucky, can you call me? Don't go trying to catch him. Only really answers to me...' Janet waved at Betty over her shoulder '...I'll come and see you next week Betty, if I can get away.'

'Yeah, see you next week. And if I see your Bucky...' the words seemed stuck in her throat, but she managed to utter them '... I'll make sure I let you know!'

Betty waited under the porch until Janet had made her way to the 701 at the end of the drive. She continued watching until Janet became part of the heatwaves forming at the limits of her vision, a quivering ghost returning to her place of haunting. Soon Janet was just a blur on the horizon, and then she vanished, consumed by a trick of the heat.

Betty turned inside. She searched out the handle for the interior door and pulled it shut, peering through the gap all the while, ensuring that Janet hadn't doubled back.

As the door closed, Betty reclined against it, taking deep breaths.

Her heart had been pounding in her chest for the entirety of their exchange. She remained leant against the door for a while, as though she were barricading it against a brazen thief. After a while, her heart rate slowed and she relaxed.

'Time to get to work...' she muttered. 'Let's see if we can get you fixed up, shall we Tom?'

CHAPTER THIRTEEN

Betty sat at her wooden dining table, which was littered with candles. With no electricity, she had to do what she could to light the place up, as night descended like a veil and the cold crept up from the depths of the earth where it had been hiding.

She reached up and mopped her brow with a handkerchief. Usually, once the sun had gone down, Juniper cooled in the shade of the mountains, but tonight as she sat there diligently toiling, surrounded by candlelight, she was working up a real sweat, of hard graft.

Next to her on a rickety chair was her sewing kit, stored in an old wicker hamper that one of her children had discovered in town one year. It'd been thrown out with all the other rubbish but they'd seen the beauty in the discarded item and brought it back to Betty.

Betty reached into the basket and pulled out her fabric scissors, holding them up to the light. She opened and closed them: *snap-snap*. After turning them over in her hands, rubbing a finger along the blade to check they were still up for the task ahead, she placed them next to the outstretched legs of the ginger tom.

The table was crowded, not just with candles, but with shaving foam, razors, thread (which dangled freely from its spool), tissues, and a bottle of Scotch – which she'd half-drunk already. She poured herself another large glass, inhaled deeply, and pulled the legs of Tom toward her. He was laid out on the table like a sleeping baby, flat on his back, legs akimbo and loose to the sides, exposing his rather large testes.

'What a big boy you are...' Betty muttered, as she played with his penis; she let it hang there, thick and throbbing, her mind wandering. She'd been so lonely... She very suddenly reminded herself to focus on the task at hand, to complete what she had set out to do. She reached under each leg and gripped him around the hips, her face inches from his balls and large flaccid organ. She pulled, dragging his hefty, muscular frame toward the end of the table. It was hard work, dragging such a dead weight. Getting him up onto the table originally had been easier: he was docile but not unconscious, hopping up with a wince onto the table as his shattered legs tried to support his weight. He was a fighter, a strong beast. Now he lay like a corpse, tongue lolling out of his mangled jaws.

'Right, let's get started!'

CHAPTER FOURTEEN

After Janet left, Betty had set about getting Tom ready. She'd soaked some stale bread in Scotch then rummaged through her drawers for some painkillers. She'd been prescribed opiates for her hip and knew she had a few still lying around. Eventually, she'd found the little white and red capsules. She'd split them, spilling the fine powder within, a pink chalky substance that reminded her of sherbet.

She'd added a little Scotch to create a paste. When the paste was ready, she'd added it to the bread. She'd shaped the soggy bits of soporific wheat into mushy balls, taking a swig of the whiskey herself to steady her nerves. She'd need her hands to stop shaking if she was going to do a good job. She'd looked down at the plate. There were seven potent balls, enough she'd hoped to knock him out whilst she stitched and splinted this broken thing back together.

She'd poured more Scotch into a large bowl of milk, warmed it over the fire, and then set about getting him to eat and drink: he'd woken during her fumbling, so she'd decided to up the dosage, and hopefully this time he'd be out for the count.

BETTY LET his legs hang over the edge of the table. He was such a large specimen that although his hind quarters were hanging off the table he still seemed to be taking up the majority of space; her candles, along with her rudimentary tools and salves, stuffed wherever there wasn't him. Betty lifted each of his legs and positioned them on to upturned brooms, which she secured in place, the handles leaning against the table. As she placed the legs onto the brush heads, it was as though they were in stirrups; it looked just like the photos she'd seen in the library.

She sat between them like a doubtful midwife – except instead of delivering babies, she would be removing the possibility of there ever being any. She moved the slops bucket with her good leg, her toes curling around the handle, pulling it toward her from under the table. She laid hold of the bucket and set it directly below his hanging testes and penis.

Betty reached under one of his splayed legs, grabbed a tumbler and took another gulp of Scotch. She'd drunk so much that it didn't even burn her throat any more. She placed the glass down and then picked up the shaving foam can, spraying the contents into her open palm, where peaks of white foam appeared. Betty massaged it into the ginger tom's genitals and up his powerful thighs. Betty felt a flutter of excitement as her fingers brushed his private parts, hidden within the blanket of white foam.

Shaking slightly, despite the Scotch, she picked up a nearby towel and wiped her foamy hands on it, then flung it over her shoulder like a barber. She picked up the razor and began shaving the thighs first. The hair there was long, snagging every now and again, until she shook the blade in the bowl of water at her side.

The water had icebergs of white foam floating across its surface, with ginger tufts swirling between them. Betty took her time shaving the tom's balls. They were slippery; the task reminded her of getting plum tomatoes out of a can. After about twenty minutes, pulling the skin taut in various directions as she used the blade, the site was clear. Shaved clean and smooth like the chin of a teenager ready for prom.

She stood for a brief moment to inspect her handiwork, tilting her head to the side to get a better view. She moved to check his pulse, leaning over his body, and felt a shock as her thigh came into contact with his hard balls. She placed a hand to his throat, fingers checking for a pulse. She didn't actually know what she was doing, she'd never had to find one before, but she could feel something beating below the surface. Betty lifted one of his heavy eyelids, the whites of his eyes scaring her slightly, and she recoiled. After a few deep breaths, she regained her composure.

It was now or never.

Reaching forward, she grabbed one of the testes in-between her thumb and middle finger. She squeezed the sac and with her index finger pushed on the hard lump within. It moved under the pressure. Her thumb and middle finger came together, trapping a flap of empty skin between them. She took up the scissors.

She took a deep breath, steadied herself, and then snipped the rubbery flesh held between her fingers. The skin dropped, like a minuscule flesh-coloured kippah, into the bucket with a wet slap and a tinny echo, reminding her fleetingly of the town's renowned pea spitting competition, and the sound those peas made when they hit their targets.

Betty wasn't prepared for the blood. It gushed out of the opening. She pinched the wound and it seemed to abate, oozing slowly out, dripping into the slops bucket. Betty calmed herself with further deep breaths. She felt dizzy, but this wasn't a time to pass out. It was a time to press on and get this over with.

She thought back to the instructions she'd read in the library, playing them over and over again in her mind's eye. Next was removing the testes from the sack. She manipulated her ring and little finger, slowly sliding the hard teste out of the incision she'd made. After some fiddly effort, a yellow sac peeked out.

She felt like a midwife, seeing a baby's head crowning. Carried away, she unconsciously applied too much pressure, and the teste popped out. It hung there on a cord of grey and white sinew whilst blood continued to trickle into the bucket. She froze, just staring at what she'd done, the prize hanging there like an eye that had been taken from its socket. She now had two hands free to continue with the next step: tying and severing.

It was the most complicated part of the procedure. There were two options, but Betty decided to go for the easiest one. She grabbed the hanging teste in her hand. It was hard like a marble. The cords seemed to retract at her touch, trying to withdraw back to their resting place. She needed more to work with, so gave it a tug; she'd seen how long they were in the photos, so pulled with all her might. Tom flinched, and she stopped; craned her neck up to see if he'd come around. He was still unconscious, tongue stuck out and saliva puddling beneath his lips.

She pulled again and his knees jerked. The cord seemed to go deep within. He was like one of those toys with a pull-cord that performed a little jig when you tugged on its string. She tugged again, just to see his feet and legs contract. They bounced up and down as she pulled, a good six inches of cord to work with now dangling from the sac.

She wrapped the teste around the cord and then popped it through the grisly loop she'd made. Once through, she pulled it with her other hand and it formed a knot of pink and white ribbon, like the red and white pole you'd see outside a barber shop. She repeated it three times, the knots glistening and sliding together. And then the teste lay in the palm of her hand like a skinned lychee, a triple knot tied above it.

Pleased with her work, she picked up the scissors. They were slippery in her glistening hand, but she managed to steady them enough to cut the now slowly greying mass from it berth. It fell with a hard thump and tang into the bucket. No sooner had she cut it from its place than the cord disappeared up into the vacant sac, retreating and defeated.

She sat back to admire her progress. The skin of the ball-sac, all pink and shaved; it looked like a baby bird calling out to its mother to feed it worms. She felt sorry for Tom.

She grabbed the needle and thread and began to suture the skin together. She'd opted for a peach-coloured thread, as it was the only thread she had that remotely resembled his pallor. She pushed the needle through the skin, then pulled the thread taut, holding the needle in her mouth whilst she tidied the stitch. She'd always been a perfectionist when it came to needlepoint. After a few more stitches and a variety of knots, the job was done.

Betty sat back, picked up her glass of Scotch and took another deep gulp. She had a lot of work to do.

She reached forward and grabbed the other one.

CHAPTER FIFTEEN

'Cigarettes are like women, the best ones are slim and rich… and well, you're neither. You're pathetic.'

The words stung when they had escaped Klein's mouth. They lingered still like a poison, occasionally bursting out of Janet's unconscious to plague her waking mind. She couldn't shake them, and they would play over and over again, each time like a plaster being ripped from a wet cut.

She stood in front of the mirror, swigging from a bottle of moonshine, three quarters empty now. Her hands trembled as she picked up and held the sharp needle to her eye. The thread drifted below it like a colourful streamer, snagging on her eyelashes. She gingerly moved her other hand up to squeeze the cut together, her fingers pinching the torn and bruised flesh, the swelling bringing out her pores; it resembled the flesh of an orange.

The blood that slowly trickled down her face stung her eye, like citrus. She took another swig of the moonshine, dulling the pain, and giving her Dutch courage for the task ahead.

Janet put the needle in position and began to push, the skin stretching under its progress. The point eventually pierced her, a sliver of metal appearing like the dorsal fin of a shark gradually cutting the surface of the water. She continued to pull and push the gleaming silver point through. Taking a break, a deep breath, and another swig from the bottle, she then began working on the adjoining layer.

Klein had dished out another expression of his love on Janet's face after she returned from Betty's. Before she'd even gotten near home, she'd begun to fear the worst. She'd been gone too long, the sun falling from the sky and Klein bound to be home from whatever appointments he'd had that day, which consisted of where he'd be able to find a place to drink and an ear to bend. His food was not going to be ready, the kitchen would still be a mess, and his appetite for destruction would need sating in some way or other.

Janet forced the needle through another few layers of skin. The moonshine was taking the edge off, but she was pretty much used to the pain by now, as well as having to fix her face with needle and thread. She only had white cotton available, so her eyebrow looked as if a caterpillar had crawled up there and started spinning a cocoon.

Janet tilted her aching neck back, checking her handiwork and Klein's heavy-handedness.

He'd been furious when she returned late from Betty's.

'Where the fuck have you been? I git home to find half of Juniper on our fucking doorstep. Queue of folks snaked right from the front door, down the stoop, and on out down the drive, all the way down to the fucking mailbox...'

He'd lit a cigarette mid-conversation.

'...all hungry, hunger burning holes in their bellies, clutching handfuls of cash. Handfuls of fucking cash! Said they'd been waiting for hours. Had to give some of them water. You know how much water we have? Not enough, that's how much. I had to give 'em summ'in though, didn't I? Bad for fucking business if the clientèle pass out from heat exhaustion.' His eyes had narrowed. 'All 'cos you were too busy traipsing your skanky ass all over town trying to make friends with that old hag Betty.'

Janet thought that the big issue here was that Klein had had to do some of the work. He'd been knocked off his throne, temporarily in the gutter with the peasants, and there was nothing more rage-inducing to him.

His usual contribution was to sit in the shade of the porch, sipping on something cold. Janet thought about the way he drank: sticking the whole neck of a bottle in his mouth and then slowly moving his mouth up to the tip of the bottle, as though he was sucking someone off. If he ever found out she thought that, she'd get a beating as bad as the one that put him away – there wasn't much that Klein hated more than homosexuals, and being referred as one would be a case worse than death, for him and the one uttering the slur.

He'd often say: '*If you have a dream where you wrong me, you'd better wake up and apologise!*' Janet knew she'd heard that phrase somewhere else, but Klein wanted to claim it for himself, and she knew better than to question him. He'd use it in front of the rare house-guests they'd have, as though it were a joke. After all, it was usually followed by laughs.

But Klein had been fuming, Janet was secretly happy that he'd had to do some work for once. It was a hard fight to keep the glow of pleasure invisible from him, however. Any flicker or facial twitch that could be misconstrued as a smile would end up with a hurt that she didn't want. In fact, he'd probably kill her.

Klein had droned on and on, informing Janet that he'd had to hold shop, deal with the enraged customers. He'd had to take 'hundreds' of orders, trudge over to the barn in the heat, carry back the skinned cats. Plus, he'd had to get them all fucking water, of course. *Now you know how I feel,* Janet had thought to herself. But her face had betrayed nothing.

She mopped at her face with a wash flannel. It came away bloody. She rubbed, suddenly feeling an insatiable desire to rid herself of the reminders of everything Klein had done. Try as she might, the bruise would not vanish. In fact, her efforts irritated it, swelling the blemish.

Wasn't this like something from a play? Lady Macbeth! That was it. The murderess had tried to scrub her hands clean of the blood and guilt. Janet smiled bitterly; she was the antithesis of Lady Macbeth, trying to scrub her body of someone else's sins.

She mopped the small trickle of blood from around the cocoon on her eyebrow. She glanced down at the sink. It resembled a battlefield hospital: blood spattered sink, tweezers, scissors, bandages, needle and thread. Was she winning or losing? Sometimes, she didn't even know what front she was fighting on anymore.

Janet recalled what had happened at the tail end of the crowds leaving her property (nothing like the *hundreds* Klein had mentioned). There had been dirty looks and knowing faces. They seemed to know what was waiting for her just as well as she did. Had Klein been boasting about what he was going to do, she wondered? And if the crowds did know, why did they just stay silent about the systemic abuse she faced? *Because Juniper is a backward town*, the answer came with no little fury. *A place of maggots and dust.*

Cowards.

After Klein had given Janet the riot act, he got up, sucking on his bottle, and moved into the house, leaving her on the stoop. He removed the cigarette from his mouth and held it out in front of him, as if he was contemplating what to do with it – whether to throw it into the brush or use it to mark her flesh again.

'You better get, woman. Dinner needs making, and I need a shower after all that covering for your lazy ass.' Klein flicked the glowing ember of his cigarette into the bushes at the side of the porch. 'Cigarettes are like women, the best ones are slim and rich...and well, you're neither. You're pathetic.'

Klein disappeared inside the house.

Janet stilled herself, took a deep breath, standing at the entrance as if it were the gates of hell. Could she run? She didn't have anywhere to run to. So, she shuffled forward into the house, the place she feared the most. Each hesitant step seemed to bring her closer to the inevitable, inescapable punishment she knew was waiting inside

– but she was drawn to it nonetheless, like fire to an arid landscape. She walked in and closed the door behind her.

No sooner had the door closed, she turned and walked straight into a boot. Klein had kicked her straight in the stomach; the air was driven from her lungs. She hunched forward, her throat and lungs screaming for air that was not forthcoming. A pain ripped through her abdomen, her hands clasped around her stomach, her body curled like a foetus.

The knee that swung up from Klein did the rest of the damage, connecting with her face. Her head flung backward, blood arching in the air like a red streamer. It seemed to hang there, glistening in the fading light, before descending on her body and the floor boards. Janet briefly thought that it was more mess she'd have to tidy up before Klein descended on her with a flurry of fists. She wasn't sure when she passed out.

She awoke to the smell of burning. She'd been told that stroke victims smelled burning, and she wondered briefly if that was what had happened. Then it all started to come back to her. She reached up and touched her sticky eye, removing her hand to see it was covered in blood. She'd been out for a while. Her blood was clotted in ruby lumps, the consistency of jam.

The burning smell continued to irk her sinuses. She thought that Klein in his rage might have decided on burning the house down, with her in it. She staggered to her feet, partially blinded, her right eye sealed shut by the swollen wound. Her feet felt heavy, not her own. Like a double amputee with phantom limb syndrome, she struggled forward, trying to get control of her weak legs.

Janet clutched the wall for balance, leaving red smears across the wallpaper, something out of one of those horror films Klein loved so much. Blindly, she searched the house for the source of the fire. She seemed to have a heightened sense of smell, maybe because it was so hard to see through blood and injury, so she moved from room to room, searching for the source by scent alone.

When she found what she was looking for, she collapsed into the chair at the kitchen table, an ever-tightening rage within her. On the table, in the kitchen, was a metal trash can. Flames licked at its sides, orange tongues from hell, flicking in and out like a snake's tongue.

Janet's good eye became glassy, tears falling. Something within her cried out to extinguish the fire, but she couldn't move. She was broken. The weight of everything that had happened pinned her to the spot.

There was a note, scrawled in pen on the back of an overdue notice next to the trash can.

Don't think I didn't know...you been getting ideas above your station.
Don't even think about going back to that old hag's house, coz I'll
find you!
You need correcting, we'll make a start when I get back.
Did you think I wouldn't find it?
Klein

Her Bible burned, words vanishing beneath flame.
Janet wept.

CHAPTER SIXTEEN

It had been a few weeks since Betty had performed her castration on the ginger tom. The weight shifted in her bed as Tom pulled himself up, latching onto the woollen blanket and heaving his reconstructed carcass onto the layered bedstead. Betty felt his weight on her legs as he managed to circle a few times to get the blankets just right. Betty felt his splinted limbs through the sheets, the sharp pieces of wood stabbing through the blanket and pinching at her thigh. She shuffled over to make room. Tom sank into the trodden-down sheets and his laboured breathing started.

'*I wonder when Janet will be popping by again?*' Betty thought to herself, their recent meeting playing on her mind.

'We'll need to be careful, won't we?' she offered to the night, knowing her new friend wouldn't and couldn't reply – but sometimes it felt good to utter words into the constant silence of her household. Tom stretched out a large paw and laid it on her stomach. He was communicating. More and more with each passing day.

His legs were mending well, and Betty was giving thought to taking the splints off in a week or so, to see how the bones had mended. She'd been able to manipulate the bones back in place, suturing the many wounds on his body. She'd even been able to give some attention to his face, but it was still like a bunch of puzzle pieces that didn't quite fit together. Now she'd cut his balls off, he was more docile and placid than ever.

Tom lay there all night, rattling, his breath caught in his throat. His breathing sounded like her husband's old harvester: gently purring away in a low gear, before suddenly jumping and spluttering as it ran low on gas. It seemed regulated by his dreams, his worst rattling always as he slipped deeper into a dream. In a way, it was relaxing; it helped her sleep, but tonight the thought of sleep was far from her mind.

Betty had been thinking of Janet. Their last contact had left an unshakeable imprint on her. She'd wake up thinking she'd been scalded by a ghost in her sleep.

She shuffled over to the other side of her bed. Tom was now sprawled out over one side and she didn't want to wake him. Betty pulled the sheets back and swung her leg out. She lifted her tired frame up into a seated position, then reached under her lame leg and swung it out to join the other.

The nights were the worst of times for her hip; being off it for so long, she'd wake and it would feel like a rusted clothesline. She'd need to manipulate it, crack off the rust before it could swing freely. As Betty placed her feet onto the floor, she jumped back in shock as one of them splashed into a cold puddle.

'Oh, not again Tom! I thought we'd sorted this out?' She spoke in a hushed voice, as if she didn't want to let the words escape her mouth and wake him, but her annoyance allowed it to sneak out into the frigid air. Her breath was a cloud of white in the dark. She leaned over to her nightstand, grabbed the small metal candelabra, reaching out again to lay hold of the matches. Betty struck the match and the room bloomed into a soft orange glow. The wick caught and soon the light illuminated the darkness. She peered down to the floor and noticed that Tom must have knocked over her evening cup of prim-rose tea.

'Well, small mercies...' she proffered. Betty thought about mopping it up now, but decided against it, her hip still aching and not yet ready to bend. Tom would probably see to it when he woke, or the heat of the day would probably dry it up by mid-morning.

Betty should have known better – the diapers that she'd bought were doing a sterling job as she house-trained Tom, but they were more to stop him scratching at his stitches, opening himself up again. He'd already gone through so much; he didn't need a return journey to the kitchen table, and neither did she.

She walked from her room, the glow of the candle flickering around the her. She watched Tom lying forlornly on the bed, his muscular body rising and falling slowly; found herself laughing at his diaper, her hairy little fella, lying there without a care in the world. It all looked rather peculiar, this large beast reduced to incontinence. How emasculating, she thought, before covering her mouth, lest another laugh wriggle its way out. She left the room as Tom began to stir from a dream, his forlorn legs twitching as if he were running through the corn fields.

Betty made her way through to the kitchen table and sat with some difficulty. She'd become frugal over time, eating little, still making her way through the remnants of the feline delicacy that Janet had dropped off. She'd been right, it had the consistency of jerky: chewy and sinewy in texture. Betty grabbed some of the flesh, put it in her mouth, moving it into her cheek like a hamster, as if she was chewing tobacco, a pastime she'd given up a long time ago now. Her fingers returned to the plate; she flicked the bones around with her finger and her thoughts turned back to Janet. Was the reason she'd not seen her because Janet was plotting revenge? Had she seen the tom? Was she biding her time before coming back and dishing out her justice? Would she be bringing Klein with her?

The long days cooped up inside the house were tedious, blurring one into the next. Betty feared even stepping outside, what with Tom growing in strength by the day. How long before he was discovered? He still needed help getting about at the moment, as the splints were still on, but he was half limping, half crawling around the house. Every now and again, he'd get his splint caught in a loose floorboard or trapped on the edge of a door and he'd be unable to free himself until Betty stepped in. Still, he was healing faster than she could have hoped, given her rudimentary medical skills.

But Betty couldn't shake her worry over what Janet might have seen. She'd had a good old peep inside before Betty found her unconscious on the steps. What if Betty's secret had been discovered?

She had been so grateful to Janet for taking the time to visit. Was she now deceiving one of the few people to show her some kindness?

Janet had been close to finding him though. Betty knew she should have reported him the moment she found him on the road, but she was so lonely. Stuck out here, without a pot to piss in, was it too much to ask for a little companionship? No, she had to stay strong and focus on not getting caught. Besides, Tom seemed to like her – otherwise he'd be trying to escape into the wild with each chance he got.

Betty turned to look at the window when she heard a scraping sound. Had someone snuck up on the house? She scanned the windows, and found no one. She was a little disappointed. The source of the sound then became clear: Tom, dragging himself across the floor, his splints scraping across the floorboards. As he got closer, he lifted his head, his face furry and covered in scars, the deepest of which ran from the corner of his mouth up to his eye; an old wound which contorted his face into a permanent snarl. He'd lost most of his teeth: those left were little white shards, sharp and shattered.

Betty marvelled at her needlework. Tom had a slight overbite now, but he was able to chew food again. He'd quickly finished off the remains of the feline surprise, which Betty had placed on the floor. Betty didn't have the heart to tell him what it was or where it came from. He'd also taken to chewing on bones, sucking out the silky marrow. Sometimes he even crunched them up, though how she wasn't sure, what with his shards of teeth. She suspected that it was probably one of the reasons for his rapidly returning strength.

Betty patted her lap as he turned to her. Tom reached up, dragging himself up onto her. The rest of him was splayed out across the sofa. She stroked his body, running a hand through his ginger hair. He began to murmur under her touch, his breathing becoming light, but his body still heavy. He was putting on weight: another sign that Betty was doing a good job nursing him back to life. She looked at his legs, remembering briefly her friend June, who had callipers as a child. The kids used to laugh and point – until she got older, blonder, slimmer and shed the mechanical legs, also growing a pair of enormous breasts. After that, they still used to point, calling her 'juggasaurus', but they weren't really laughing *at* her anymore.

Betty placed her hand over her home-made callipers, as her fingers ran over the bolts she'd used to make them structurally stable. She glanced at Tom, who lay with his head on her lap, sleeping.

'Everything's going to be okay! We'll get these off in a day or two and see how these legs have mended... Mama loves you!' Betty bent down and kissed his scarred brow. It felt like kissing the strings of a tennis racket.

The weeks turned into a month, Tom getting stronger all the time. With his training wheels off, his legs seemed to have mended very well indeed, although he now walked with a limp, letting out small whimpers when the pain got too much. When that happened, he'd opt to crawl along the floor, dragging his hind quarters like a corpse pulling itself out of a grave. Betty was feeling the pain herself, each time she moved, shards of agony chasing up her leg into her spine. She hadn't been able to leave the house to pick up her prescription for a few weeks for fear that someone might come knocking, and most of her supply she had given to help Tom with the pain. She was also worried about Tom becoming inquisitive about the outside world, and about his burgeoning strength, too. He might try to flee if she didn't keep lavishing attention on him, and then she'd have no one.

They spent their days huddled up on the couch. Holed up in the sweltering house, as if they were awaiting the oncoming apocalypse –

which, with the unrelenting heat, they could well be facing. At least, they'd have company.

The days seemed to billow and sag around them, claustrophobia setting in but both too weak and in pain to even attempt to go outside. Even if they did, in their state, they'd fall lame and dehydrated and the sun would burn their flesh from their bones.

They had each other, and that was enough for now. It would be enough for eternity if Betty had her way. It was like living inside a hastily constructed house made of sticks, their sanctuary liable to collapse in on themselves at any given moment, should someone come knocking.

Then it happened: the moment she'd been dreading, but knew would be coming.

'Betty, you in there?' The knock came again, more forceful this time, and Betty thought of her stick house falling down around them. Tom lifted his dozy head from Betty's lap.

'Betty, open up, I've gotta speak to you?' It was Janet. Betty thought about staying put; moving was going to make her feel as if she had pins in her hip. But she knew that Janet would soon move around to the side windows and start peering in as she had done before.

'I'm coming! Give me a moment, hip's giving me some gip!' Betty put a finger up to her mouth as Tom glanced up, all glassy-eyed and fearful. She lifted his head off her lap and stood, frantically looking around for a place to stash him. For all she knew, Janet had figured out that she'd had him here all along. What had she seen when she'd been peering through the window all those weeks ago?

A saucer on the floor?

A trailing leg?

Bloody tissues?

It was too much to bear, so she quickly shooed Tom off the couch. He slumped down with a yelp, his legs still brittle, but Betty helped drag him to the larder. It was the closest room, with a single small window high up near the roof. Betty also thought that there would be no reason for her impromptu guest to venture anywhere near there.

She stuffed him inside, his limbs folded under himself. Tom looked at her, his face hard to read, shards of teeth bared; Betty assumed it was fear etched over his jigsaw-like face. She reached down and patted him on his head, ruffling his hair.

'Mama's going to be right back, you stay quiet now, ya'hear?' She closed the door, locking Tom inside, and staggered toward the front door. On her approach, Janet knocked again.

'Betty, please, someone might see me!'

Fat chance, Betty thought, as her hip made a grinding noise with each step. No one comes out this far.

'I'm coming, dear.'

Betty got to the door, sweat dripping from her brow, the pain like a hot poker in the flesh at her hip. She staggered slightly as she approached the door, placing her hands in front of her to steady herself. She reached for the handle, her hand slipping off the hot metal, as though unwilling to face what lay beyond it. Rubbing her hand over her dress, she tried again, this time turning the knob successfully, a crack of light appeared around the door.

'I thought you were never going to answer...' Janet said.

Betty pulled the door back further, the light spilling into her house like a home invader, the heat an unwelcome accomplice as it bustled through with a mind of its own.

Janet rushed in, head covered, looking like a nomad, a drifter in the desert, the heat pulling at her shape so that she was like a warped reflection in a curved mirror. Betty closed the door.

'Drink?' Betty offered, as Janet removed her shawl.

'That would be lovely. Thank you.'

'I see you've dressed for the weather today...'

Betty wandered into the kitchen, using the walls and cabinets to help her walk. Janet followed her, close as a shadow. Betty filled two glasses with water, breathing deeply. *Any minute now she's going to mention it.* The thought kept repeating, an internal mantra. She turned and placed Janet's glass on the table, lifting her own glass to her mouth, hands shaking, water giggling around inside. *Can she see me shaking?* Betty wondered. She took a deep draught.

Betty's glass tumbled to the floor, shattering. Glass and water spilled across the stone floor.

'What happened to your face?'

'Oh this...' Janet said, lifting a hand to her cheek. '...it's nothing, why don't you sit down?' Janet waved Betty to the chairs in the lounge. Betty thought it sounded more of an order than a request – and in her own home, it just felt damn right odd.

'I'm okay here, I think ...' she offered.

Janet reached into her pocket and pulled out a gun.

'I think it would be best if you take a seat.'

Betty didn't take her eyes off Janet. Janet waggled the gun to the side to get Betty moving. Seeing the gun, seeing Janet hurt, Betty realised things had gone too far. But she wasn't about to give up without a fight: she needed Tom, she loved him even, and she wasn't about to just hand him over. Betty shuffled into the lounge, stepping as carefully as her hip allowed over the glass on the floor. She sat down in the armchair as Janet followed, gun trained on her. When Betty was settled, Janet took a seat on the sofa.

'Sorry, where are my manners...' Janet placed the gun on the wooden coffee table. The sound reminded her of when her husband used to bring in pieces of engine and dump them on the kitchen table. Janet leant back in her chair, her face sharp and edgy, shadows falling in all the wrong places from the light cast from the window: edges visible that weren't there last time she'd visited. Janet looked Betty in the eyes and smiled a sad smile.

CHAPTER SEVENTEEN

Klein pulled up outside the house. He sat in the car for a moment, peering out through the dusty windshield, watching the cats hunting – observing as they jumped in and out of the corn like little jack-in-the-boxes, flying through the air and plucking the greedy mice from the stalks. The field was alive with them. But Bucky was still elusive, still out there somewhere.

There had been no new reports, no sightings – nothing from the posters that he'd put all over town. Bucky could even be dead for all he knew. He watched the cats a little longer, wondering if another would rise up and become the stud of the farm, have their pick of all the pussy on offer. But they all appeared to be young and sleek. Nothing like the behemoth of a creature that, if he was honest, scared even Klein. He'd hated having to go out to the barn and check on Janet, just in case Bucky was out there, staring at him, waiting for him to let his guard down so it could take a swipe. Klein was pretty sure that Bucky had an unhealthy attachment to Janet, some strange predatory instinct. Did Bucky in some way think that Janet was another of his clowder? Or perhaps the creature sensed her fear whenever he was near? Animals had a strange way of picking up on fear; it made them strike out. He didn't fancy falling foul of Bucky, so more often than not kept his distance.

He took one last look around the tall corn field, wondering if Bucky were lying in wait out there. When nothing materialised, he stepped out of the truck, from the frying pan and into the fire.

He opened the door. He was expecting the smell of dinner cooking, the sweet scent of fried meat - life. But he couldn't smell anything, just a damp, dusty odour. He moved from room to room, methodically checking in each one. He removed his bag, which was hanging over his shoulder, and dropped it onto the kitchen table. He moved to the cracked kitchen window Janet had yet to fix since the bird had hit it. Klein, of course, had better things to be doing with his time. He peered through the splintered glass, a spiderweb frozen within the pane. He waited, but after not seeing anything moving in the barn, turned and walked to the lounge.

'Janet?' he called out.

There was no answer. He moved through the house to the bathroom. Nothing. She wasn't anywhere in the house. He reached into his faded jeans pocket and fished out his cell. Sweat rolling down his face and collecting on his stubbly chin, then dripping off onto his shirt.

He pressed call.

Waited.

Her phone began to ring.

It was in the house somewhere. He followed the noise into the living room; on the shelf, Janet's cell flashed and vibrated.

'Stupid fucking woman. Why'd she go leave her fucking phone?' He picked it up and a piece of paper fell onto the floor. Klein threw Janet's phone back onto the shelf and stooped to pick up the paper. It was folded over many times. He opened it up and saw it was a letter.

Klein, I've left. For how long I don't know. I just needed to get away for a while. Please don't try to find me, I've left my phone so you can't speak to me.

I don't want to be contacted.
It's for the best...I love you Klein and I always will - but you're going to
do something one of these days which there is no coming back from.
You'll kill me. I'll be in contact soon. Janet.

Klein's hands trembled with rage. He crushed the paper and threw it on the floor. The sound of its impact was small, pathetic in contrast with what he felt growing within him. He grabbed a picture frame from the shelf and stared at the picture of them both, standing outside the house when they'd moved in. He placed his thumb over Janet's face. Pressed down until the glass cracked. When he removed his finger, her face was smeared with blood.

He lifted the frame up and then brought it down on the corner of the table, smashing the frame to pieces. Klein screamed into the empty room, like a wounded animal.

He overturned a table: glasses, vases and flowers flying across the living area. He picked up a wooden chair and thrashed it around, smashing everything in the room, until he was holding a broken club of a leg. He'd laid waste to everything. His body expanded and contracted with his rabid breaths, a hulking mass of furious rage. Then he heard it.

Something was vibrating. Was it Janet? Had she seen the error of her ways? Was she calling to say she'd made a terrible mistake? He stepped through the carnage, a wartime medic stepping over corpses and debris to see if he could find anyone breathing in the wreckage.

He lifted up the collapsed shelf and there on the floor was Janet's phone. A mobile number flashed on the screen.

It was a number he didn't know. Was this the reason she'd left him? Had she been unfaithful? His rage surged again, but he mastered it. He knew how, because in prison there was always a bigger bastard than you, and sometimes you had to swallow your pride to get your revenge.

He picked up the phone and tried not to shout into it.

'Who is this?' Klein was out of breath, his voice deep as a bear growl. As the other person talked, his mask of rage softened, turning into a smile. 'Right, I see, on the 701... and when did you last see...' He was cut off by the person on the other end of the phone. 'I'll head out soon...'.

Klein hung up, a smirk pulling up the corner of his mouth. He wiped his forehead with the sleeve of his shirt as his breathing returned to normal. He waded through the broken memories that littered the living room.

As he continued through the house, he realised he was still clutching the broken chair leg in his hand like a bat, his fingers and knuckles turning white around it. He walked to the front door, swung it open and stared out into the failing light. He still had a couple of hours before it was truly dark.

'Where the fuck are you? Where the fuck would you go, and who the fuck would take you in...'.

In the distance Klein could hear a car approaching. He stepped out onto the porch and around to the side of the house facing the road. He stood there drumming the bat on the balustrade. Watching the car speeding along the 701, a cloud of red dust thrown up into the air in its wake. It continued past, not even stopping when it hit one of the cats that had ventured out into the road, flinging its body into the air. It spun and landed with a sickening thud. That's when an epiphany hit him with the same bone-jarring force.

'Betty...'

With that, he was off at a canter, down the rickety steps. A cat moved towards him, perhaps seeking a stroke, trying to rub up against his legs. He swung the club low. *Crack!* It sounded like someone had just hit a home-run. He'd crushed its skull. The twitching body lay on the gravel behind him.

Klein hoped Janet would come quietly, without a fuss, as he didn't know what he was capable of now. He was, for the first time, scared of himself.

He spat on the floor before clambering into his truck, wiping his mouth with the back of his chubby hand. He threw the bloodied bat into the footwell on the passenger side and climbed in. Placing both hands on the steering wheel, he let out another scream. The car rocked back and forth where it sat as he pounded the wheel. He caught sight of his eyes in the rearview and saw only bloodlust there, a milky tear dribbling from his cloudy eye.

He put the keys in the ignition, slammed his foot on the gas. Wheels spun on the gravel, dust pluming and cats skittering away into the field as his truck sped off down the drive like an engine straight out of hell.

CHAPTER EIGHTEEN

The horrors of war were real. The shell-shocked woman sitting before Betty was ghostlike, a husk of a life. Betty struggled to look at Janet; there were just so many scars. A sob came to Betty's throat unbidden: an ugly, deep wracking sob. Janet watched her crying without an ounce of change in her expression.

Betty moved to pick up her drink, the drink that Janet had got her. Janet flinched, her hand snaking to the gun still lying between them on the table, and Betty thought better of it. A door slammed down the hall, buffeted by the draught coming through the open window. Janet's black and bruised fingers gripped the arm of her chair.

'It's just the draught, dear...'

Janet scanned the living room, like an assassin counting the exits. Betty reached out a hand. Maybe she could offer some comfort, like she had done before? As Betty's hand made contact with Janet's skin, Janet darted toward the gun still resting on the table. Betty withdrew instantly. Janet's flesh felt leathery and coarse, like the skin of a kiwi. Scar-tissue.

'Don't touch me!' Janet whimpered, her voice breaking. Then suddenly she looked weak, drained, as though even creating sound seemed like a chore. Betty held up her hands in a 'surrender' gesture. Janet inched back, like a sea-snake withdrawing into their cove.

Janet finally returned her hand to her lap, though it still fidgeted, itching for the gun, missing its contact.

Something had died, though what it was Betty couldn't tell. Was Janet ashamed? Had reliving some of the pain of her relationship caused her to crawl back into the pit of despair she had only just managed to free herself from? Betty gradually leaned forward, ensuring to keep her movements slow and deliberate.

'Janet?'

She noticed Janet's cold dark eyes – flitting around the room, avoiding eye contact as much as possible. Betty couldn't help but think how much Janet looked like a mouse, her gaze stopping every now and again, usually on some stain or dirt. As Betty followed that gaze, she realised what a pig sty she'd been living in.

Scratch.

It started off quite quietly. The scratching could be mistaken for a rodent, rummaging around in the larder, but with the deathly silence that had descended like a cloud on the room, it gained a weight and significance beyond itself.

Janet grew more and more on edge with each note: twisting her head on her little neck like a barn owl looking for the source of a sound.

SCRAAAATCH.

'Betty, what the hell is that noise?!' Betty sat there, thinking fast on what to say.

'I can't hear anything, dear, might just be the wind or mice?' she offered '...you see we don't get many of your cattle out this way, so the mice have been having a field day.'

Betty could feel herself going red, her cheeks flushing. She quietly hoped that because the house was like a furnace her flush could be mistaken for heatstroke.

'It's coming from in there...' Janet pointed into the kitchen '...I'll take a look.'

'No, no, it's fine dear, honestly, you sit there... I'll check it out! I'll be right back.'

Betty stood, hoping that the gun was for protection from Klein rather than for inflicting pain on her. She lifted her weight using the arm of the chair – her leg had seized up from being seated for so long – and began walking towards the kitchen.

'Well, only if you're sure.'

'It's probably just the wind, dear.' Betty said again. She hobbled into the kitchen, taking fleeting glances over her shoulder ensuring that Janet hadn't followed. Or worse, picked up the gun. She used the kitchen table and the sideboard to manoeuvre around the kitchen more freely, as an ape might use tree branches. She got to the larder door and could her the muffled sulking of what lay behind it.

As Betty moved closer, she noticed the shadow shift under the door. Tom was right up against the wood, no doubt pining for release. Betty had to open the door quickly and place her body within the jamb to ensure that Tom didn't sneak out, make a bolt for freedom. She reached a trembling hand forward and clasped the hook, which locked the cupboard. When it was unhooked, it swung low and tinkled lightly as it swung back and forth. Immediately, she felt a weight against the door.

Betty took a final look at Janet, who was now leaning forward, her bony broken digit fingering the trigger. Then she spun the gun around on the table. Playing with fire.

Betty turned back to the door and slowly began to open it. She shoved her foot in the gap, quickly followed by her knee, then peered inside. Tom pawed at her leg, then stretched up, his limbs almost reaching her chest, using the shelves for purchase. Betty batted him off and he collapsed back onto the floor, a knowing look on his scarred face.

'You just behave yourself! If people find you, you'll have to go away and I won't get to look after you anymore. Do you want that?'

Betty saw his head droop, as if he were moping. He seemed to understand, shuffling his body in a circle and collapsing back onto his side, his head resting on a bag of grain.

'It'll be over soon, I promise.'

She closed the door.

'What's going on, Betty?' Janet's voice was close. Betty turned to see she had snuck into the kitchen, displaying some of the qualities of the ghost of a person she was becoming. Betty fumbled with the hook as she slammed the door and began to usher Janet back into the lounge. As Betty half escorted and half pushed Janet back into the lounge she failed to realise that the hook made no purchase with the loop and it swung freely.

The shadow visible beneath the larder door shifted again, moving towards the unlocked door.

As Betty and Janet moved into the lounge, they stopped short: both hearing a car pull up outside, the gravel shifting under its hastily applied breaks. They froze. Beneath Betty's fingers, Janet's skin seemed to become clammy, and she started shaking.

'It's him!' she said.

A door slammed. Footsteps marched across gravel, military-sounding.

Thud.

Thud.

Thud.

There was a loud bang on the front door.

'Janet! You in there?' Klein's voice was venomous, as if his spit could turn milk sour.

Betty squeezed Janet's arm. Janet turned and Betty put a finger up to her cracked lips. Janet's eyes were glassing over, filling with water. Her pupils had gone so small they were almost nonexistent, only two little pin pricks of black in a sea of green remained.

'Betty, you in there? I know you're in there...you've got nowhere else to go...is Janet with you?' The last part was laced with a slyness that made Betty's skin crawl.

'What are we going to do?' Janet said, in a hushed voice.

'Just ride it out, girl. If we don't let him know we are here, he'll just go away...trust me.' Betty matched Janet's tone.

'But what if he....' Janet's words were cut off by another tirade of fists pummelling the door, rattling it within its frame. Janet flinched with every blow, imagining his fists finding her again.

It stopped as suddenly as it started: Klein's footsteps were heading away from the house. The two women inched through the house to get an eye-line on the door. The shadow underneath was retreating, allowing more light in.

Then the shadow paused, contemplating its next move.

Maybe Klein had even been fooled into thinking no one was in? Betty grew hopeful. Then the shadow lurched to the left. Just in time, Betty dropped to the floor, pulling Janet down with her. Betty thudded to the ground, her hip sending searing pain up through her body; it erupted from her mouth in a strained yelp. Janet shook beside her like a cat that had just been rescued from a drowning. Their eyes locked and they both seemed to reflect each other's fears.

Klein padded around to the side of the house, appearing menacingly at the window, his face dulled as they viewed it through caked dust. He reached a hand up and began rubbing at the pane until the dust flaked off and smudge cleared. Janet was breathing fast, rodent-like. Betty put an arm around Janet and pulled her tighter.

'Just stay down...he can't see us here...' Betty uttered.

'What do we do?' Janet whispered back.

Betty stifled another groan of pain. They watched Klein's shadow intently as if an apparition had appeared on the floor. Slowly, the shadow began to peel away from the window. Klein's afterimage grew smaller and smaller, until he disappeared completely. They couldn't hear any footsteps, just their individual hearts beating in their chests. The sound in their ears of blood rushing, like an ocean.

As Betty began to right herself and Janet rose from behind the sofa, they were sprayed by a hail of shattered glass. A rock flew through the air and bounced off the table.

'Hello, you little bitch...' Klein had appeared at the small window, an evil rictus on his face '...you forgot to hide the fucking gun!' Klein glared at the gun, then back at the women. Somehow, it still felt like they were the ones trapped in *his* sights. 'Wait till I get you home!'

He placed one pudgy fist into his other pudgy hand, cracking his fat knuckles, then darted away. Janet began to shake uncontrollably as if she were in the throes of a seizure. Betty grabbed her by the arm and tried to pull her away. She was immovable. Betty pulled with all her might but couldn't budge her; it was as if her feet had grown roots and they had worked their way through to the foundations of the house.

That was, until the door caved in.

Light spilled into the house as the door broke under Klein's rage. It hit the wall and started to close again before he lifted one fat hand up and stopped it swinging.

He was a silhouette suspended within a frame, sun spilling in around him.

Janet lunged for the table, grabbing the gun. She appeared to be muttering something under her breath, words of encouragement perhaps – Betty couldn't make them out. Klein took a step over the threshold, whistling an eerie song as he came. His shadow reminded her of that film with John Wayne, the closing shot of *The Searchers*. It'd been one of her husband's favourites.

Janet raised the gun with both hands, perhaps summoning every last drop of energy she had left to keep it trained.

Klein turned the corner, staring down the barrel of the gun. Betty cowered behind Janet. Klein tilted his head.

'Ahhh...look at you two. You make a right sorry pair, don't you?' he spat.

'Don't come any closer Klein. I mean it...!'

'You mean what, precisely?'

'I'll shoot you.'

'You won't shoot me.'

Janet pulled the trigger. Klein screamed as the bullet went clean through his upper chest. Blood sprayed down his shirt and trousers, spattering over the wall behind him. For a moment, they thought he would fall. But then they saw his eyes. Wild eyes. Coke-fiend eyes. The eyes of someone with nothing to lose but everything to gain. The eyes of someone whose body would keep dancing long after it's dead. He came at them, swinging a heavy fist, knocking the gun clean out of Janet's hand. A second shot rang out and somewhere, something smashed.

The blow sent Janet stumbling, but she righted herself.

She shifted backward, reaching behind her, trying to shield Betty from the pain she knew was coming. The women skirted around the table, bringing them closer to where the gun had fallen. Janet glanced at the gun on the floor. Klein noticed and began to circle back around the table, forcing the women to retreat away from the gun. He looked like a zombie, lurching with every step, the hole in his chest like a keyhole to peep through. But Janet knew he could still kill, even leaking red as he was.

A sadistic game of cat and mouse was unfolding.

'Where did you get that anyway? Take it from my drawer when I was sleeping, did ya?' Klein stooped down, keeping his eyes trained on the women, his fingers groping until he felt the coldness of metal — blood gushing freely from his chest, painting the floor red as he lifted the gun from the floor. He swung it around, pointing it at the women.

'Ha. I aint gunna shoot ya....' Klein laughed manically. 'That would be too easy for you stupid bitches!' He tucked the gun into the back of his belt. He placed the fingers of one hand around his wrist and twisted at the joint. 'They say working with your hands is good for the soul, after all!'

'Klein, Betty has nothing to do with this!'

Klein had never heard her talk so freely.

'Remember who you're talking to! It's been too long since our last correction, hasn't it, Jan? Guess you've forgot your fucking manners!' Klein feigned to go one way around the table and then sprinted the other. His dummy sold the women, throwing Betty off balance. Janet bumped into her in their haste to evade the onrushing Klein.

He grabbed Janet's hair, pulling it hard toward him. Janet's neck snapped back and all of a sudden, she was Klein's possession again. Betty threw herself at Klein, hands around his face, scratching at his eyes and cheek. With all his might Klein swung his thick arm up, connecting with Betty's face. The force of the blow sent her reeling into the table edge, her hip connecting with a *crunch*, the momentum carrying her over the table. Betty hit the floor, her head bouncing off it, blood pooling around her face.

'What have you done!?' Janet screamed. 'Betty! Betty can you hear me?' He pulled her head back, as if preparing to sacrifice a goat, then reached his free hand around and began to close her windpipe with his thick, bloodstained fingers.

'Why Janet? Why did you betray me? You were the only one waiting for me when I was locked up. The only one I thought I could trust? Why Janet? Why?' Tears ran down his face. Janet's breathing had all but stopped, black spots appearing in her vision.

Then he relinquished his grip on her hair and reached into his pocket. He slammed her back against the wall, still applying pressure with his fingers on her larynx. With his free hand, he lifted his phone to his ear as if this were just a normal afternoon – without a care in the world.

'This better be fucking important' Klein barked.

Janet's vision slowly returned as Klein's grip loosened. She glanced down to Betty, a pool of blood surrounding her head. Betty had not moved since she hit the floor.

'Yep, I understand. I'll be there soon. I'm just sorting out something... I'll call you when I'm on my way. Keep an eye on it. Whatever you do, don't fucking lose it!'

Janet noticed a metal jug on the sideboard next to her. It held flowers, long dead, succumbing to the heat like the rest of the town. Slowly, she wrapped her fingers around the handle, feeling the weight of it as she did.

Klein replaced his phone in his pocket, his thoughts somewhere else.

Janet smashed the jug against the side of his face, cracking him across the temple and jaw. The implacable grip Klein had on her throat was broken. Janet heaved in much-needed oxygen, feeling dizzy and light.

Klein stumbled backward, falling against the larder, his back and then his head rattling off the door. It clattered; the lock, hanging loosely, swung. His legs crumpled and he fell in a heap on the floor. Janet bent over, her hands on her knees, breathing deeply. She lifted a hand to her throat, touched the burning skin there, more bruised flesh.

She looked back at Klein, picked up the jug and walked over to where Klein lay.

His face is a bleeding mess. His chest is a bleeding mess. Somehow, he still isn't dead.

'Now, Janet...'

She lifted the jug and kept swinging it. The jug acquired dents under the force of the blows. Each time it returned a little bit bloodier.

When she could do no more, Janet stepped back and dropped the jug. Klein's face was a crimson mess, barely human. *Like his fucking soul,* she thought, with beautiful savagery. Janet rushed to Betty, lying on the floor.

'Betty? Betty?' Janet rolled Betty onto her back. There was a deep cut over her eyebrow, open and wide. 'You need to get up Betty. Wake up! We need to get out of here!' Then, almost like an afterthought. 'Out of fucking Juniper!' Janet tapped Betty's face.

Betty began to stir, Janet pulling her to her feet.

A gargled moan almost made her drop Betty. It couldn't be, but she knew it was. She looked back at Klein's body. He was sitting up, shaking his head as though shrugging off a heavy night of drinking, blood spattering the walls like water; a dog shaking off its fur. His hands went to his face, confused by the fact he couldn't see out of one eye, his milky eye leaking grey clods down his cheek. His good eye met Janet's. There was no hate within his gaze now; even that had been burned away. Now, there was an emptiness that frightened her more. Groggily, he gripped the larder door and kitchen counter, lifting himself slowly.

Janet was sure now that Klein was unkillable. Perhaps that was what going to prison did to you.

'Betty, come on!' Betty stood on unsteady feet, blood obscuring her vision. Janet saw a knife on the kitchen draining board and picked it up. She held it in the direction of the wobbling Klein. 'Get away!' she shrieked. 'Get the hell away!'

She jabbed at him, one arm looped around Betty's back, supporting her.

Klein stumbled away from the knife, hitting the larder door.

'If you come near me, I swear to God I'm going to stick you with this! I'll fucking kill you, you hear! I mean it Klein! Stay where you are!' Janet started to manoeuvre around the table, helping Betty, heading toward the lounge.

'We don't got time for this nonsense, Jan,' he said, as though they were merely having a disagreement about pricing on their cattle. 'Look what you did to me?' He sounded incredulous, more impressed than anything else. 'Do you know who that was on the phone?'

'I don't care! Let us go!'

'It was Brandenburg! Says he's got Bucky!' The smile that Klein offered was full of blood.

'Bucky? Where?'

'Said he found him in his outhouse. Been hit by a car, he said. He's walking lame! So, we are going to stop this shit: I'm going to tidy myself up and we're going to go get him.' Klein extended a hand. 'Come on, Janet. Fair's fair. You got me. Now, let's get Bucky. Our boy!' He grinned, took a step forward. Janet sliced the air with the blade. Klein stepped back.

'I said I'd kill you. I mean it Klein...'

'Not if I kill you first, you dumb bitch...' Klein pulled the gun from his belt. He rubbed at his gummed eye, but it wouldn't open.

Janet and Betty froze.

'I tell you what, Janet,' Klein said, all niceties dropped. 'I'm going to shoot that stupid hag first. She's got you thinking you're somehow better than me! You can watch her die, then we can go pick up Bucky...'

Klein lurched toward Janet and Betty. The door to the larder began to slowly open behind Klein, swinging on its hinges.

'Step aside, Janet...'

'No!' Janet could see the door to the larder gradually opening. There was something in there, a shape. It might be enough, just enough, to distract Klein.

'You both need to leave...' Betty's voice wavered.

'What?' Janet spun to look at Betty.

'You both need to go... You need to get out of here now. I won't tell anyone...'

'Showing your true colours now, Betty!' Klein sneered.

Janet looked incredulous 'Betty, you know I can't leave with him!'

'Trust me... you need to get out of here.' Her voice had shrunk to a whisper.

Klein lifted the gun, pointing it squarely at Betty.

'Klein please... please don't...' Betty averted her eyes, as though by doing so she could avoid the bullet that was coming to her.

'What the...' Janet had seen what was behind Klein. A shadow had begun to stretch out from within, its shape spreading across the wall behind Klein like mould. A hand gripped the door frame, a faded Confederate flag tattoo on the dorsal aspect, its bony fingers latching onto the edge of the door. Janet took in a sharp breath, turning to Betty.

'What the hell is –'

Klein turned just as the shape exploded from the door. It descended on Klein like a vengeful fringe, fast and feral, smothering him, its mouth snapping away. Klein wrestled against it, but Tom was latched on like an octopus, his legs wrapping around Klein's waist.

Klein thrashed, knocking into the kitchen walls, gun still in hand trying to get a shot.

Amidst all the confusion, Janet was struck by the absurdity of whatever this creature was – this creature wearing nothing but a diaper. And then, just as quickly she was drawn to its face; distorted, broken and fused back together, but somehow the mouth and shards of teeth still working, snapping chunks out of Klein's flesh. Overpowering the flailing arms, teeth found Klein's neck. Blood poured from the incisions, splashing down Klein's chest as he let out a cry of rage.

'Get the fuck off me!' Klein used his gun like a club, slamming the pistol-grip into the monster, but Tom didn't seem to register the blows.

'Betty, what *the hell* is that? What have you done?' Janet yelled.

'I found him by the road: he was almost dead... I... I... helped nurse him back... I just wanted to...'

Before Betty could finish, a gunshot broke through the air. Janet and Betty hit the ground. Another shot rang out and a window shattered. Klein fired blindly at the thing clinging to his back. Tom clawed at Klein's already bloody face, opening wide his milky remains of an eye with a raking slash. Dug his fingers and nails into the bullet wound in Klein's chest. Klein's screams filled the air.

'They're killing each other....' Janet screamed at Betty. Klein fell to the floor, blood dripping from more wounds than could now be tallied, his swollen eye a grey, weeping crevice. More blood trickled from his neck onto the floor.

Tom pinned Klein, and for a moment the monstrous man was confronted by Tom's hideous face staring straight down at him. Klein's gun-hand was trapped by Tom's powerful leg, the gun now pointing toward Janet and Betty.

The gun went off as Tom plunged his teeth into Klein's exposed windpipe. The bullet struck the table near Janet's head, splinters flying; she let out a scream.

'I'm sorry Janet...' Betty said. 'I had no idea – '

Tom twisted, and Klein's finger twitched again. There was another shot, and Janet dropped to the floor. Utterly still.

'No,' Klein said. There was a scream coming, but it was cut short as Tom finally tore through the hidden gristle of Klein's throat with an audible crunch. Klein twisted his gun-hand loose, shaking as Tom continued to chew on his innards. He gasped, bubbles swelling in the hole torn in his oesophagus; they bloomed and burst like monstrous balloons.

Tom lifted his head, as if sniffing the air, and turned to glare at the stricken Janet and the bloodied Betty. He shifted his weight, still on all fours, and took a tentative step toward Betty. Blood dripped from his mouth, and he spat out chunks of flesh onto the floor.

'Janet... Janet?' Betty scanned Janet's prone body, looking for the bullet-hole. She lifted up her arms and could see blood on her top; the bullet had hit Janet in the side. Betty rolled her over, using all her might, and found there was an exit wound too. Betty needed to stop the bleeding and get her out of here.

Tom dragged one of his legs behind him, damaged further by the struggle with Klein. Betty looked at him, his brown, almost black, eyes staring back at her. His expression was hard to read, but it was almost as if he was asking if he'd done a good job. Klein was beginning to stir – though how was anyone's guess. Horribly fitting. Like an insect robbed of most of its body, but still somehow able to move. She turned back to Janet, who murmured something.

'She's alive! Tom, she's alive!' Betty saw what she imagined was a smile appear across his broken and distorted features. Behind Tom, Klein had rolled onto his side, gun raised...pointing directly at Betty.

'If I can't have her...' Blood spluttered from his mouth.'... then... neither... can... you!'

Klein pulled the trigger, releasing his final bullet. Before Betty could react, Tom stumbled in front of them both. Betty flinched. A cloud of blood, like mist, covered her, cold like an April shower. She opened her eyes, hands searching her body, looking for the wound.

She lifted her gaze to see Tom lying in a crumpled heap on the floor, the top of his head missing and leaking greyish-red fluid.

Her heart was finally broken. Tears formed in her eyes, dripping down her cheeks. She reached out a hand and rested it on Tom's outstretched hand.

Janet moaned as she started to wake. Klein's powerless body lay on the floor: dead at last, gun still clutched in hand, blood pooling around him as though someone had taken out the cork keeping it all inside.

'Janet! Janet! Wake up!' Betty shook Janet's arm.

Janet's eyes opened, like stuttering blinds.

'Thank God, you're awake!' Betty lifted Janet's head and began to cradle it in her lap.

Janet's head lolled to one side, seeing the carnage before her. Her eyes fell on Klein's body. She began to heave, her body rocking back and forth in Betty's arms with uncontrollable sobs. She turned away, as though unable to bear the sights. Betty held her like one of the daughters she'd lost so many years ago.

'Wh...wh...'

'Don't worry Janet, just be still, it's okay...'

'Who was...?'

Betty sat, frozen.

'It wasn't meant to be like this', she implored, to no-one.

F

CHAPTER NINETEEN

The town now survived on roadkill, and that is what brought Betty to the 701 today. She'd had rich pickings of late, since the cats were now running wild.

After the incident at Betty's, Janet had released Juniper's livestock. She'd opened the doors to the barns and let them run free, drawing a sorry line under that whole season of her life. People asked after Klein. Janet had told them that he just took off, and when he didn't return, they stopped asking. His memory soon disappeared into the history of the town: just another resident who'd upped and left, fled or escaped.

They weren't surprised that he'd left Janet, and people knew she was better off without him, but they never voiced their concerns, preferring to stay silent as they had always done.

When Janet eventually went to the Brandenburgs' to tie up loose ends, they couldn't find Bucky. Janet had initially gone to euthanise him, but he'd managed to escape by tearing a hole in the shed that they'd trapped him in. The will to live was strong with him; he'd never go easily.

Now, Betty hobbled down the edge of the 701, pushing her

wheelbarrow, her head shrouded with a shawl to protect her balding scalp from the heat of the sun. Clouds were rolling in too, big and menacing, causing the air to become somewhat like a sauna after someone had dropped water on the coals, the hot air trapped with nowhere to go. '*It was black over Bob's mother,*' as Betty used to say before a storm.

She dripped with sweat, beads of it snaking down from her head and over the ragged scar on her brow - a constant reminder of her run-in with Klein and the aching loss of Tom. It stung at her eyes.

She was in search of the latest victims of fast cars and careless drivers — the tourist trade trying to get through town as quickly as they could to sip sangria and feel the sand between their toes at the beach two counties over. But something about today felt different.

In the distance Betty noticed something large on the roadside. It wasn't moving, but it was big, curled up on the side of the road. She stood there, hands on her hips, surveying the scene before her: it felt all too familiar.

'What is it, Betty?' Janet's voice called out from behind her.

'Looks like we'll be eating well tonight Janet...' Betty pointed towards the shape on the side of the road.

'Wow, that's a bigun, aint it!' Janet exclaimed as she crested a small mound by the roadside.

They headed down the 701 toward the shape on the ground. They could hear a distant rumble coming from behind them. They needed to act quickly. Whatever was coming was big and fast. They moved around the body, which was covered in mange, ginger tufts blowing in the hot breeze.

'It's him... ain't it?' Betty offered to Janet who was staring down on the beast before them.

'Yep, that's him... that's Bucky alright.' The sound grew closer, seeming to move the air around them.

'Right, let's get him loaded into the barrow... before anyone else claims him.'

Both of the women bent down, lifting the huge, heavy carcass into the barrow.

The noise they'd been hearing, the slow rumbling in the distance, was now on top of them.

As they dropped the forlorn body into the barrow, thunder broke out and rain began to fall. They both looked up to the sky, feeling warm splashes of water land on their faces for the first time in what seemed like forever.

With the next rumble of thunder, the women stared into the darkening sky, in awe of what they were witnessing. A blinding crack of lightning soon tore through the darkening sky; they continued to stare into the abyss above them, as Bucky's leg twitched in the wheelbarrow.

ACKNOWLEDGMENTS

Sadie Hartmann (Mother Horror) thank you for championing this book from the get go, and for believing in my words it is truly humbling.

Daniele Serra, your work on the Hardback edition of this book is insane, like my crazed town! You have singlehandedly given this book and this series the epic makeover they needed and rightly deserved.

Chad Lutzke, thank you for your friendship and your awesome cover design skills.

Ryan Mills - thank you for crafting such beauty from my macabre words!

Special thanks to David Eagleman for his permission to quote his fabulous words from 'Metamorphosis'.

I wanted to also thank the hugely supportive BookTube / reviewing community out there, who have taken me and my crazy books to heart - you know who you are, I appreciate you all greatly.

And lastly, thanks to you, dear reader. I hope you've enjoyed Juniper and that you'll stick around and discover the other books in the Juniper Trilogy as well as my many other works.

But for now, thank you!

ABOUT THE AUTHOR

Ross Jeffery is the Bram Stoker and 3x Splatterpunk Award-nominated author of Juniper, Tome, Scorched, Only The Stains Remain, Beautiful Atrocities, The Devil's Pocketbook, Milk Kisses & Other Stories and Tethered.

Ross' fiction has appeared in various print anthologies and his short stories and flash fiction have been published in many online magazines.

Ross lives in Bristol with his wife (Anna) and two children (Eva and Sophie). You can follow him on Twitter here @RossJeffery_

9 798355 106317